The Shepherd's Hut

Also By Tim Winton

TIM WINTON

The Shepherd's Hut

PICADOR

First published 2018 by Hamish Hamilton, an imprint of Penguin Random House Australia

First published in the UK in 2018 by Picador
an imprint of Pan Macmillan
20 New Wharf Road, London N1 9RR
Associated companies throughout the world
www.panmacmillan.com

ISBN 978-1-5098-6387-7

3 5 7 9 8 6 4 2

A CIP catalogue record for this book is available from the British Library.

Printed and bound by CPI Group (UK) Ltd, Croydon, CR0 4YY

IN MEMORY OF

GILL DENNIS

Change is slow and hope is violent

LIAM RECTOR
'Song Years'

I

Whe n I hit the bitumen and get that smooth grey rumble going under me everything's hell different. Like I'm in a fresh new world all slick and flat and easy. Even with the engine working up a howl and the wind flogging in the window the sounds are real soft and pillowy. Civilized I mean. Like you're still on the earth but you don't hardly notice it anymore. And that's hectic. You'd think I never got in a car before. But when you've hoofed it like a dirty goat all these weeks and months, when you've had the stony slow prickle-up hard country right in your face that long it's bloody sudden. Some crazy shit, I tell you. Brings on this angel feeling. Like you're just one arrow of light.

And bugger me, here I am hitting a hundred already and still not even in top gear. On squishy upholstery, with one of them piney tree things jiggling off the mirror. I'm flying. And just sitting on me arse to do it. Off the ground. Out of the dirt. And I'm no kind of beast anymore.

So what does that make me? Someone you won't see coming, that's what. Something you can't hardly imagine.

Say I hit your number, called you up, you'd wonder what the fuck, every one of youse, and your mouth'd go dry. Maybe you're just some stranger I pocket-dialled. Or one of them shitheads from school I could look for. Any of youse heard my voice now you'd think it was weather. Or a bird screaming. You'd be sweating sand. Like I'm the end of the world.

Well, no need to worry. I don't forgive you, none of youse, but I'm over all that now. You're all in the past.

Me phone's flat anyway. Plugged into the dash, charging or dying, I dunno which. So relax, I'm not calling. Everything's changed. I'm not what I was. All I am now is a fresh idea fanging north up the highway to where it's hot and safe and secret. I got someone to collect. In Magnet. She'll be waiting and ready. Least I hope so.

Fifth gear. It took a few goes to find but I'm there now. With red dirt flashing by. Mulga scrub. Glinty stones. Roadkill crows. The Jeep reeks from all them sloshing jerry cans in the back. But the windows are open and the wind is warm and the stink of petrol beats the smell of blood any day.

All of a sudden I'm hungry. I get the .410 by the neck and heave it over on the back seat. I shove the box of shells away to get at the food and it's still warm on the tin plate. It's good and greasy and tastes of smoke. From the first swallow I get a hot charge.

And I drive like that, just under the limit, with a chop in one hand and the wheel in the other. Laughing hard enough to choke. For the first time in me life I know what I want and I have what it takes to get me there. If you never experienced that I feel sorry for you.

But it wasn't always like this. I been through fire to get here. I seen things and done things and had shit done to me you couldn't barely credit. So be happy for me. And for fucksake don't get in my way.

The day the old life ended I sat up under the grandstand nursing me bung eye and hating on old Wankbag till the sun went down. Mum always went crook when I called him that behind his back. Captain Wankbag. The Captain. Or just Cap for short. Said that was no way to talk about your father, but it was no odds to me. That bucket of dog sick was a bastard to both of us, I wished he was dead. And right then I was praying for it.

Me hands stunk of meat. I made fists of them, hard and flat as sawed beef shanks. I stared at them till there wasn't any light left to see them by but it didn't matter because in me throbbing head I could see a cleaver in one and a boner in the other, feel them there real as money. Sat gripping them imaginary things so long me arms cramped up and I had to come out in the night air before I keeled over again.

It was cooler in the open. Couldn't see nothing but the lights of town. Some blokes kicked a ball way down the other end in the dark, just voices and hard thumps that gimme the yips. I didn't know what to do, where to go. Had no money. Some ice would of been good. Like frozen water ice, I mean. For the eye that was half closed over. Fucking hell, it was like something growing out the side of me head.

The sky was blank, I seen more stars when he clocked me, and I started trying to figure the time.

Before this, back in the shop, I come to in the bone crate. Woke up arse over and half stupid in that slimy pile of shins and knuckles and chook frames, and for a sec I didn't know where I was or how I got there. But I copped on soon enough. Where was I? Work of course. And how did I end up poleaxed in a bin? The usual way, that's how. He wouldn't give you the sweat off his balls, the old Captain, but when it come to dishing out a bit of biff when you weren't looking, well, then he was like fucking Santa.

I heard the radio going out front. And that lemony detergent stink was in the air. So it had to be after close-up. And now he's having to wipe out the trays and slush the floor on his own, the dense prick. Bitches all afternoon about what a lazy bludger I am and then makes sure he can't get any work out of me when there's most to be doing. No wonder he's such a big success in business.

I looked out through me knees and tried to get to me feet,

but Christ, that took some doing. Would of made a nice old picture, that. Jaxie Clackton, hardarse the kids run clear of all over the shire. Trying to spaz up out of that greasy nest of bones like a poisoned fly. Talk about laugh. But I done it in the end. Grabbed onto the bench. Pushed off the muck-specky wall. And stood there a mo with me head spinning. Probably gobbing and gawping like a goldfish. And all the time, just the other side of the partition, through the door and the skanky flystrips, the mop's slopping and the bucket's getting kicked across the floor, and he's wheezing and snorting and going on some mumblefuck about how bloody useless I am and how he's gunna flog some morals into me. And in me mind right then I was already gone. Up the street and shot through clean. But it's like I was doing everything half speed, pissing off in slow motion. And any second he's gunna come through the door and get me by the ear and give me a couple more to be going on with. So I told meself to harden up and get a wriggle on, to get me apron undone and kick off them stupid butcher boots. Not real easy, any of that, not with a woozy head and sausage fingers. But I got them off and grabbed me Vans and the skateboard by the back door and sleazed away quiet.

Outside the air was warm and the day nearly done. I peered up the street through the shadows and just to squint that tiniest bit hurt to the living fuck. When I touched me face it felt like a punkin full of razor blades. And I shoulda been relieved I was out and away but I had nowhere to go. All I wanted was a bag of peas on me face and a bed to lay on. But it wouldn't be safe to go home till Wankbag was fully rummed up. Which took some doing. He was pissed all day at work, that was just him regular. Getting himself totally off his tits, that was a few hours' hard relaxing. After a shit and maybe a shower. Rip his eye patch off and just sit there in his jocks. His empty socket sucked into a cat's arse squint. Grab a two-litre bottle of Coke from the fridge, tip half down the sink and fill it back up with Bundaberg rum.

No point me going home till he got his medicine down. He'd stagger round a bit. Park himself here and there. In the shed. Or out the patio looking at the paddocks and the train tracks. Mostly he ended up in that big rocking TV chair passed out blind, lights on, curtains open. Snoring hard enough to rattle the glass. Made it simple to figure when to make your move. Pull up outside in the dark street. Suss him through the window. Watch to see he's out properly. Then go in the back way. Take your chance in the kitchen. And get to your bedroom fast. Lock the door. Shove the desk in front. And let him sleep it off. Tomorrow'll be a new day. Which is really the same miserable fucking day all over again. Till then there's nowhere to go but the footy oval. That's why I was up there, hiding like a girl. The roadhouse was iffy and the pub was plain trouble so I had to hole up under the grandstand. That was it. And that's what I done. I took a breath of air and snuck back up under the joists where it was all chip boxes and old frangers and Beam cans.

I waited past dark and then a few hours more. I didn't dare look at me phone to check the time or see if there was messages, the light's a dead giveaway, you don't make that mistake twice. So there was nothing else to do but hang on and guts it out.

In me mind I saw him going drink for drink with himself, like he was in some kind of dipshit competition to get written off faster than anyone else in town. Sid Clackton, Bundy rum champion of the world. Captain Wankbag, master butcher, roadkill specialist, drunker than any man alive. Monkton's finest, what a mighty hero! I imagined the slobby prick frying himself a pan of bangers and yelling at the telly. Look at this fuckwit, shut your mouth, who's this ugly moll, this is bullshit. On and on. You didn't even have to be there to hear it. And I thought if only it could all be poison. The rum, the beer, the meat, the bloody air he snorted. If only he could fucking die and leave me be. If there's a God out there why can't he do the righty for a change and kill this cunt off once and for all. Because all a person wants is feeling safe. Peace, that's all I'm after.

Well that's what I told meself. But that idea got old. Pretty soon what I really wanted was a few bangers of me own. Fucking peace could wait. I was hungry as a shark. And now I thought about it I didn't want to still be out there at closing time when half the front bar spilled into the park for more. I sure as hell didn't want to get into it with any goon-drinking darkies or the apprentices from the John Deere. I had no fight left in me, so I figured enough was enough.

I come out from under the old wood grandstand and listened for anyone out there on the oval. But it was quiet. So I stuck the skateboard under me arm and snuck across to the trees round the boundary and stayed under them till there was a streetlight and some bitumen. Then I rolled home the back way.

It was all pretty chill up our street. A couple of windows with telllles flashing in them but nobody outside that I could see, no porch-smoking Paxtons, no Mrs Mahood standing there with the hose the way she does all day.

Our place was dark mostly but I could see light spilling out from the open doors of the shed and I heard the radio going. And I stood there a sec on the drive where the light didn't reach and tried to steel up for it, figuring better to go in now than have him come and find me standing in front of the fridge. It's always best to be ready.

I headed for the shed and then I stopped. And I dunno why really. Just peered inside. All I saw was his ute. That shelf against the back wall piled with camping gear. The big globe hanging off the truss with a few moths clattering about it. I thought maybe he was in there tapping a drum of homebrew. But it was a weeknight. And whenever he pulled the pin on a batch the whole street give off the sour reek of beer and he got suddenly popular. It sure as hell wouldn't be this quiet. Even if it was only him and the copper drinking it, they'd fill the place with all their bloke noise, ya-ya-ya, mate, yeah fark orf, and there wouldn't be that meaty smell I was whiffing right now. I knew he still took sly beef from blokes passing through and he had a chiller room off the side to keep it all clear of the shop, but the doors were wide open and he wasn't so thick he'd leave it like this, not even if he was expecting someone. And there was something funny about his ute parked in the shed. From out on the drive I could see the Hilux was way too high in the arse, like the tray was all angled up.

I flipped the board a couple of times and let it fall to the cement to show him I was there. I guess I could of called out something or coughed the way people do but he'd of heard me already. For sure. If he was in there, that is. Odds were he was waiting, foxing, messing with me. Like it's his fucking hobby, giving a dude a nervous breakdown.

So I went in careful, with the deck of the board like a shield in front.

And I thought, I'm not seeing right. Because of the swollen eye.

Maybe that's why I didn't cop on straight away. Because the front wheels of the Hilux were fully off. Both of them was laying flat on the floor, one against the other. The nuts in a pile next to the wheelbrace.

And the hubs. Fuck me, the bare hubs were down hard on the concrete. And the ute was casting a shadow that no light was ever gunna make. A shadow doesn't search for a drain like that. Shadows don't have blowflies drowning in them. But I spose for two seconds I let meself think it was just oil. Like he'd dropped the bung out of the sump, too pissed to remember to slide a drain pan under it. From the corner of me good eye I could see the half empty bottle on the bench. No bubbles left in the Coke. Something sucking at the open neck, a wasp maybe.

But I still didn't really know what I was looking at. Until I crept up past the driver's side door and peeped over the bonnet and saw his hairy legs and his bare feet stuck out from under the roo bar.

I dropped the skateboard and it scooted away and hit something with a clang and then I saw the high-lift slumped away from the vehicle. It was laying across rags and a tarry puddle on the cement. I saw tracks where some lizard run through the mess on his way out the door. And then it was plain as dog's balls. I didn't even get down on me knees and check. Maybe I should of to make sure and take some satisfaction from it, but I already knew the old turd was cactus. And it's not as if I was crying any tears but it knocked me. I had to lean against the Hilux to keep meself up.

Me head was everywhere and nowhere. I mean, Jesus. But after a bit I started having proper thoughts. Like, the doors are wide open. And by eight in the morning the Cap won't be at the shop and by nine someone's gunna want to know why they can't get a porterhouse and the bag of snags they ordered. I sure as hell wasn't stopping round to have half the town point the finger at me, saying I come in and caught him when I finally had the jump on him. People knew I had good reason, it was no secret in Monkton how he was and what he done to us. They'll say I kicked the jack out from under the roo bar and crushed his head like a pig melon. It all points to me.

So I turned round and walked out real careful not to step in anything. Left everything like it was. The radio going with some angry old prick barking stuff meant nothing to me.

The lights blazing away.

I went straight for the house up the side path. But I had to stop for a sec. Near the gas bottles. Yacked all over me Vans. Puke the colour of mustard it was. I just kicked them shoes off and kept going.

Dark in the house. I found the switch in the kitchen and when the fridge kicked in I jumped. Christ, the state I was in.

Went into me room, took down me pack from the wardrobe. Looked at the swag but knew it was too big to carry. Pulled hunting clobber from the wardrobe, the camo pants and jacket. Nearly tripped and fell getting the dacks on, I was in such a hurry. Took the pack to the kitchen and filled it with tins and packets and stuff from the fridge. Took the stove lighter. Three boxes of matches. Wrapped it all in tea towels to keep it from clanking.

The big bedroom stunk of him but it still hadn't quite give up the smell of Mum. Stood in there a mo just looking. Then I got the key that was hid up behind the doorframe. Unlocked the gun safe with it, took out the .243 and two boxes of shells, Winchester 80 grain soft points. Took the binocs as well.

Halfway down the hall I turned round and went in the bathroom. Snatched a bog roll and forgot the toothbrush.

Out in the laundry I found me steelcap boots and yanked them on. Hanging off the trough was his blue singlet, Y-fronts, a striped apron stiff with fat and blood. Just stared at them while I laced me feet in. Like those stinking rags might leap at me on their own, even now.

Then on the washing machine I saw the water bottle he took

to work every day. A five-litre Igloo. Figured I'd be needing it. Filled it from the tank outside and tried not to think of his filthy mouth on the spout. I knew there was a coupla camel-packs out in the shed. One of them'd be ten times better than lugging a jug, but I wasn't going back in there for love or money. Which was a big fucking mistake, I'll give you the tip, bigger than the toothbrush and it cost me hard the next few weeks. But I topped the Igloo up and the brass tap give a yelp when I shut it off and when I was done I walked round the side of the house, stood under the big old flame tree a minute, getting me breath and me wits, and a roadtrain come by, taking the back way to the servo, hissing and jerking to keep his speed down, all lit up like a ship and reeking of wool on the hoof, and once he was gone I took a good look round, stepped out into the empty street and walked fast as I could.

There was no one at the oval still. Nobody that I could see, anyhow. I cut by the changing sheds and was out into mulga inside two minutes. Just a bit of moon now. Enough to see the shadows of trees and tell what was clear dirt and what was bush.

I reckon it was half an hour before I lost the lights of town. I thought that might be a good feeling but it was lonely. I coulda cried. I mean I was happy, wasn't I? It was just sudden.

I told meself this was the best day of me life. Figured by morning I'd fucking believe it.

Being a cheap bastard is what killed him.

All that brake trouble he was having with the Hilux and he won't take it up the road to Cec Barton. Reckons he'll do it himself. Except his trolley jack got flogged back in March along with the compressor and the bunky crossbow. Coons, he said, but really it coulda been anybody.

So he cranks the thing up with a high-lift under the roo bar. And any fuckwit can tell you that's not smart. You never get under a vehicle hanging off one of them widowmakers.

Well there's no widow. And no one's crying any tears for him. Not in Monkton, not anywhere in the wide world.

I didn't think about any of this then. I just went. Got going, kept going. That's all I was for days, this moving crazy thing. Pushing. Hauling. Going.

First two days I stayed right away from the highway, so far back you couldn't hear it or see it. Kept at it day and night. Angled north whenever I could. Tried to stay out of sight but that's a mission in the wheatbelt because there's hardly a tree left out there. Nothing but stubble paddocks far and wide. Everything flat and bare. Shanksing across that country you stick out like a rat on a birthday cake. One time, for an hour or two, I slept under a couple of wandoos in a fence corner. Just wedged in a pile of granite rocks. Daytime it was, and when I woke up there was a bird looking down on me, one black cocky giving me the stink-eye. Like what the fuck are you doing out here?

I was lucky both them days. With the weather specially.

Because it was full autumn now and I knew further south people had crops in already. But up this way the rains hadn't come and no one was seeding yet so there was hardly a bastard out there but me. No machines moving, no vehicles on the side roads. Farmers musta been in town bitching or sat in front of the telly watching footy. Maybe that's when they get on the nest, these people, I dunno. Anyway I just slipped through boundary lines, kept off the gravel and give driveways and houses a wide berth. Which isn't so hard in wheat country, out there houses are rare as rocking horse turds.

I went hard, half running if it was safe but the going was ugly. I was hauling too much stuff. It got easier as the water bottle emptied out but that wasn't gunna help for long, was it?

Second afternoon I pinched some water from a place that looked like no one had lived in for years. There was papers all stuck in the flywire door and toys on the dead lawn. It was the last house and the last farm I seen before the salt country.

Maybe I was being too careful. Could be there was never anyone coming for me. Maybe nobody was interested enough. It was only Captain Wankbag. Everyone knew what a cunt he was. But someone pegs it like that, mashed flat under a car in his own shed, people want to know the how and why and who. And there was me skateboard still in the shed, bogged in all that blood, and me spewed-on shoes on the path and the gun safe open. And who's the Captain's bestie? The cop with the gold tooth. Yeah, that fat ranga with the hissy laugh. They were pretty thick them two, and just my luck. Used to hear them out in the shed laughing like poofs over stuff I couldn't never figure out. Gotta be why he was safe all them years, and not just with the meat neither, I mean bashing the tripe out of Mum week in and week out and walking round town like butter wouldn't melt in his dirty cakehole. His copper mate, that's why she never put him in, why she never said nothing.

Used to wish Mum'd just get in the Corolla and drive down to Perth where the cops didn't know us and the bloodnut couldn't pull any moves. It's hardly four hours down the highway. But I knew the city give her the yips and I understand that. Wouldn't last a minute there meself. Still, she coulda buggered off to Geraldton. Same distance really. That's a big town and we're nothing to nobody in Gero. Just drive in there and do him up once and for good. There's a real police station and a courthouse and all. She coulda got herself a place by the sea, et prawns, got herself free. But she'd of been leaving me with him. On me own. And she knew what that'd mean. Every day she was gone, every day she was safe she'd have that on her head. Even if she didn't go to the law, even if she just disappeared, she'd know what her safety cost and who'd be paying for it. As it was, I copped it anyway but it mighta been easier to take if she'd run away. Getting the shit kicked out of me woulda been worth something then. Reckon I wouldna blamed her, not even back when I didn't know what sacrifice meant, what a martyr is. I would of took it. That's what I tell meself. I wanted her to run, I begged her to and that's the truth, but then I was glad when she said she couldn't and that's true too. I know I was just a kid then but that's something I gotta live with. I didn't get her free. I didn't have the brains. Or the guts.

I knew what people thought, but. Jaxie Clackton, that dirty fuckup. He was getting what he deserved. And his mum was just another budgie-brain female too stupid to save herself. The Cap they had to be nice to, to his fat face anyway, especially since the IGA closed. But they had him pegged. Clacktons, we were rubbish. Town like Monkton, one pub, roadhouse, rail silo and twelve streets, half of them empty, small enough everyone heard something and they all had a fucking opinion. But no neighbour ever once come running when Mum needed help. No one called the cops. Not with that great one-eyed pile of shit running amuck. Lots of big opinions in our town but when it come to saving Shirley Clackton there wasn't a ballsack in the whole shire.

She was the one with guts. Said she stayed for me. And you don't know what that's like, how something that good and pure can feel so filthy.

I come to the first little salt lakes so I knew where I was. Picking my way round them pans I had the urge to lay down in all that soft purply-pink samphire. I heard people say you can eat it. Maybe the olden time blackfellas did. Nowadays, them people, all they eat is chicken and chips.

I kept hustling north. The sun come up over one shoulder and went down by the other.

I tried to get me thoughts straight while I went. But there

was too many of them. Then for a long time, hours it was, I had no thoughts at all. And when they come back it was like fuzzy radio.

I spose it's wrong to pray that someone dies. But us Clacktons aren't churchy people and I never did any praying at all till I had nothing else to go with. I only went to church once or twice and that was pretty crap. Honest, you can see right through those people. Up at Magnet this was, when I was younger, with Auntie Marg and them. She's no churchier than the rest of us but she goes to a baby sprinkling now and then to suck up to the publican and the nobs in town. We went into the Catholics, not the mission place. She'd never go where there was people like that, the local indigenous. Anyway church was mad. Mumbo-jumbo and ladies in big hats. Everyone following along like trained monkeys. What give me the creeps was seeing how they let the padre put his soft pink priesty hands on the baby. Don't these cockheads know anything?

No, I got no use for any of that magic shit. Some jokers come to town in a little yellow bus one weekend and walked round chatting us all up in the streets and shops and down the oval. Musta been five of them in a row asked me was I saved. And I laughed in their goony-bird faces. Fuck, they wouldn't know the half of it. Maybe if they give up their Jesus talk and let me sneak on that bus they could of saved me then and there. Not that I woulda gone, not with me mum to think of, but if they only knew what kind of saving I needed it might of shut their gobs and taught them something.

Nah, I'm not the churching sort but I've thought about all the prayers. If that's what I was doing them years. If wishing and wanting and hoping so hard you sweat bullets and your balls climb up inside you to die is praying, well then I done plenty of it. And got fuck all for the trouble. All that whining and begging in the dark. It's undignified. Asking something, someone, anything, for a big black anvil to fall from the sky like in the cartoons. Kerang! On Wankbag's head. Because nothing else was gunna save us. Not unless I topped meself and set Mum free. And I thought of that a coupla times. Course I knew where the guns were, where the key to the safe was. Coulda gone and done exactly that. If I wasn't such a pussy. I prayed to be brave and I stayed scared. And then when Mum got crook I asked for mercy, to make dying quick and painless for her. But there was no saving and no mercy for Shirley Clackton. And me, the only relief I got was having the feeling flogged outta me by the Cap.

Once Mum was gone and it was just me and him I mostly give up the praying. I figured the only thing left was to kill him or outlast him. And I never had the nerve to blow him away. I thought I could never do something like that. Which just shows you. So that meant outliving him. Then bugger me if a big weight doesn't land on his head after all. What's the odds? I dunno if it's my fault or not. Like maybe the Cap did it on purpose. Could be he was ashamed and lonely or just so fucked up he didn't know what he was doing.

Or what if someone else did it? I wasn't the only one in town hated his guts. Whatever, whoever. That high-lift jack, that was me saving and me mercy.

I don't know if I really thought about all this shit while I was hoofing it north. Some of it maybe. It's hard to remember. There's gaps. Mostly I was too scared and numb to work stuff out. Them few days there woulda been dogs thinking more than me I reckon. But I did wonder about all this afterwards. Still chewing on it now, tell you the truth. Isn't that what I'm doing today, still praying, begging her to be there up the highway, hoping she'll be ready when I call? When you need something, even if it can't be got, especially if it can't be got, you ask anyway. So I figure even if you don't believe any of that crap you're always praying to something, or someone. Even when you shout at the TV, when you talk to cats and yell at cars. Hell, I've pleaded with puddles and stars and piles of rocks. Not exactly ashamed to say it neither.

But praying to get someone killed? Not much philosophy in that.

I knew one thing those first days walking. It was what kept me going after the first panic wore off. That I was it. Last man standing. Still am. Call it a stroke of luck, answered prayer. After a miracle what you end up with is me. Me, motherfuckers!

The eye wasn't too flash. I kept wanting to tip water on it to cool it off a bit but I couldn't afford to waste a sip so I kept on, sore and fat-headed, and just looked out me good eye. Kept on north best I could. I didn't have any clear plan, only getting to Magnet. But that's three hundred kays from Monkton. Making it there was gunna take some time and I didn't know how to do it yet. But right then the big thing was cover. I had to find meself some trees. And fast. Once I had bush I could move without being seen. Then there wouldn't be any hurry. I'd have time to think.

I was always gunna go north. Even if I had no one to go to. South of here it's all farmland. A few more trees down there where they run sheep and beef, but more people too. Past that it's the city and there's no way.

No one ever called me lucky but maybe I am. For one thing, Monkton's not so far from the goldfields, hardly an hour by car, and maybe that sounds like desert if you don't know any better because it is pretty rocky, that's true, but it's greener than you think. I know some of it, which is another lucky thing, something I can actually thank the Captain for. Because he did give me a few things. Flogged some hardness into me. And I can hunt and butcher. I know some quiet spots to camp too. In the gold country. Outta the way places. Where no one'd think to come looking.

When I come to this big blue line at the end of the day I nearly shit meself. It was like an army of cops waiting out there for me. I give out a little girly squeak and dived down in a ditch, face first. Got meself a mouthful of dirt and a smack in the chops from the waterjug. Just layed there panting and twisting off, trying to figure where I could bolt to. Nothing behind me but bare ground. When I got me breath back I took a peek. And saw what a fucking goose I was. It wasn't men up there, it was trees. I was that pissed off at meself. But relieved. And in the end you had to laugh.

I took a sip from the Igloo and layed back a minute. Glad as hell and all soft and gooey with it. And then I reckon I dropped off a bit. Because when I come to there was a couple of spinifex pigeons at the edge of the ditch. Checking me out. The sky behind was faint, it was nearly sundown. When I stirred them birds took off with that creaky sound their wings make. Then I got up, pulled meself together and made for the shelter of the trees.

They was jams and gimlets mostly. And kurrajongs. Nothing big. But enough to hide in. They stretched on as far as I could see. I got into them quick and walked until it was dark and I was so tired I thought I might trip and break something. But it was good to be surrounded, closed in. That night I had a fire. You don't know what a difference a fire makes. You'd think I'd found a house to live in and a shed to park me car in, I was that happy.

I et two cold chops and three baked spuds and the smell of them was on me hands all night, like when you been with a girl. And just thinking that had me turning the phone on. Which was stupid but I was messed up. I was hardly catching one bar of signal now but the light off the screen was nice.

There was no messages or missed calls. Nothing on me page, no notifications. And all the texts from her were old. I looked at a coupla photos but that killed me. I had to keep me shit together and save the battery. Most of all I needed to stay smart. It's one thing to make no calls and stay off GPS. But just switching your phone on you ping a tower somewhere and leave a footprint. Like an idiot. And the cops can probably fiddle your phone remotely anyway, switch your tracking on without you even noticing. I had to leave it off now and stay strong. But by the time I shoved it away me stoked mood was gone.

I just looked into the fire and tried to stop feeling sorry for meself. It wasn't cold and there was no mozzies. I was rooted but I was fed and I'd come a good way already. Another day or two and I might be safe.

I slept okay but I had dreams and woke up a lot. There was no wind but the trees creaked and cracked. A coupla times something give off a thud. A roo maybe. Least I hoped so. Every time it happened I sat up with me heart peaking.

Jesus, I told meself, harden the fuck up.

She heard me say that once, Mum. To me little cousin out by the laundry where he was bawling, his knee bleeding a tiny bit. She had that disgusted look on her face. What? I said. I didn't do nothin.

You're no better than your father, she said. Listen to you, Jaxie, you sound just like him.

I didn't talk to her for three days. That's how fucked off I was.

She was wrong about me. But I was wrong about me too.

You tell yourself you're not the praying type, not the kind who talks to himself or cries for his mum or gets himself torn up over some chick. You're not that sort of softcock. Not a bully neither. You just like a fight and you always did. But you're not a psycho, doesn't matter what they all think. Even if you hate someone's guts you're not the killing kind, you're sure of that. And not even in your weirdest dreams do you think you're an instrument of God. You dunno what that even means. You're a kid, you don't know anything.

First light was up when I woke. The dirt was purple. I lit the fire again to warm a tin of pork and beans and then I realized I had no opener and no knife. The opener wasn't such a biggie, I hardly had any tins anyway, but with no knife I was up shit creek fully. It was a kick in the arse. I couldn't believe I was that stupid. No camelpack and no knife, what a fuckwit.

I et some noodles dry but they made me hell thirsty so I hoed into me waterjug something shocking. Now I wished I'd gone in that abandoned farmhouse the day before and got meself a blade. There'd of been something left in the kitchen, or even the sheds. And now there wouldn't be a farmhouse between me and bloody Bali.

When the sun come up I saw there was a billion spiderwebs

all shining along the ground and across the dead timber. Like the silver lining people talk about. And I felt maybe I'd be alright. So I got up and going.

Possibly an hour out I come to a little rubbly clearing with a coupla sheets of rusty tin curled up and some twists of wire. Like what was left of some prospecting setup. Trenches and holes and small piles of stones and dirt and one half-collapsed ditch. Didn't look like anybody got rich digging and poking there. Didn't look like they tried real hard neither. But I found a bent star picket in all the crap and it was jagged at the butt where some numpty bashed it crooked with a sledgehammer, so I used it to bust into me tins. Et the pork and beans cold. Sitting in a ditch full of bottles. And it tasted pretty decent. I opened up the pineapple chunks and the corned beef and stuck them back in me pack where they wouldn't spill. I wasn't about to go carrying a star picket along as a can opener.

But then I pulled them tins out again and emptied the pack and looked over what I had. Besides the beef and pineapple I had four oranges, one onion, another packet of noodles, a lighter, three boxes of matches, two tea towels, a roll of dunny paper and the ammo. I had the glasses round me neck, the waterjug in one hand and the rifle on the strap over me shoulder. It was too much to carry but not nearly enough to keep me alive. I had maybe two litres of water left. And no hat and no knife, what a mong.

I wasn't so sure about the steelcap boots now. It was staky ground out here but the Vans mighta been easier to walk in. Me feet was sore and me shoulders too but there was no point stopping. I could go a coupla days on the food I had and maybe last a few after that but if I didn't get a drink tomorrow I was in the deepest shitter ever dug. No getting round it, I had to find a bore or a tank or I was stuffed. The chances of coming across either one wasn't real flash but if I couldn't find water I'd have to pack it in and head for the highway, flag down a truck. And then one thing'd lead to another. Any way you cut it from that point it was over.

I got going. I was that dark on meself, especially about the knife. But the anger kept me at it, going hard.

By the afternoon I could hear roadtrains thundering way off to the left of me and I figured I'd met the highway where it elbows off towards the gold country. I hadn't seen a fence in a day and a half. I was on the money. And it was no use thinking how quick I coulda come this far in a car.

Now there was just prospecting country for hundreds of kays. Maybe a broken-down sheep station here and there. Further east, far as I could remember, there was just the desert, the kind of country that'd boil your insides dry in a day. Only a proper blackfella could live out there and there's none of them left, so I wouldn't be trying it on, not even with a hat and a blade and a skinful of water.

I pushed on a couple more hours. Kept near the highway, close enough to hear a truck now and then but far enough into the trees no one'd see me. But that road started to do my head in. It was bad having it so near and I knew I should stay away but I cut over to cop the flash of roadtrains through the trees, trailers high and bright as buildings. Crept in so I could see the pearly quartz bits in the bitumen shining out there in the sun. I hunkered down in a clump of jams, right in the shadows. I could smell the tar and oil and rubber, I was that close. You could hear a truck coming a long, long way off. And when it come by, clanking and jerking, those triple trailers rumbled the ground under your feet and ripped at your hair, spitting chips and blowing past hard enough to pin your ears back. When it was gone it left a cloud of pink dust and that hundreds-and-thousands feel of diesel grit on your tongue and it took a long time for the quiet to settle in again.

I thought about all that milk and beer and meat and fruit headed north. I never been there but I pictured all them big towns way up, Karratha, Hedland, Broome, Kununurra. That's a lot of people to feed. Everything they need comes up on the road. Just one of them trucks'd have enough packed in it to keep me alive for a year. Two probably. I had a weapon, it's true, but I couldn't see meself jacking trucks. How long would that caper last? Anyway I can drive a car pretty good but I've never tried a rig with three trailers and eighteen forward gears.

I just sat there. Like hypnotized. Thinking any moment I could step out and show meself. Catch one of them roadtrains and in two days be in the full-on tropics, Wyndham maybe. Darwin. Long as I ditched the rifle someone'd pick me up in the end. But even without the Browning and the ammo I'd look dodgy as hell. Staggering out of the bush, face like a bucket of smashed crabs, stinking the way I did. And maybe I was on the news by now. Then I'd be toast. But not everyone's the good citizen type. Some truckies'll always turn a blind eye. But not for free. I lived long enough near a roadhouse to know what a ride north can cost. You think it only happens to chicks? Well I wasn't that desperate, not yet.

All the same I wasted a whole hour by that road. It was like I forgot who I was and what I was doing. As if I was alone in the world.

I had to keep my shit straight. Find water. Rest up. Get to Magnet. Otherwise I might as well pack it in and die. So in the end I got up and got on with it. Took meself deep into the bush and put the road behind me.

Thing is, I'm not alone in the world. That's the only thing keeps me going.

I dug right into them scraggly trees. Stepping careful through the million sticks and strips of bark in the shadows because getting snakebit wasn't gunna be any help.

I got someone. And that means something. It's why I was back thinking of that shady pub verandah in Magnet, them long curtains. Smell of bore water out in the yard behind.

Soon enough I couldn't even hear the highway anymore. The air was warm and mad with clickers and bees and hoppers. For a while I tried to figure what all that sap and tree oil smelt of. And then I got it. It's like what your mum rubs on your chest when you're little. Vicks. In the smeary jar.

I didn't stop all the rest of that day. I was dry and tight in the legs but away from the road me head felt clear again. That's when I started thinking about her. Lee. Reckon I thought about her more than I'm letting on but it was something to keep the nasty shit away.

See, it was the middle of the afternoon, school would be getting out. She'd be hauling her bag home down one of them wide empty streets on her own. I hoped she was pushing her board with the new wheels and trucks I give her. Maybe she never got them, I didn't ever hear. Abecs, they were. Pink SickSicks. Cost me four weeks' pay. I don't care, it was worth it.

I followed her home. In me head I mean. To the pub. Upstairs. I could see her in the shade, on the big verandah. Reading a book, or with her buds in. We like prison books. And thrash. Well the books she reads and tells me about. The music we listen to together, sharing buds.

It was warm now and I figured it'd be hotter still up her way. Maybe she'd go down the pool. I could picture it easy. The crazy blue water. The soft grass where we layed our towels. Bleach smell of her hair up close.

I wished to fuck it was wildflower season. So I'd have something to give her when I got there. But there wouldn't be any flowers out here till September. If I showed up with anything it wasn't gunna be wildflowers, that's for sure.

They said it was a good season up here last year. First winter with any rain for ages. People turned up like locusts. City people. Tourists. Asians and all. They never stopped in Monkton for anything except pies and petrol. Nothing to see in our town but farm wives and browntooth drunks. But those weeks I watched them coming and going. Sat outside the roadhouse just to get a good look and laugh at them fuckwits.

Not that I got any beef with people going to see wildflowers. Used to go along with Mum up this way some years when I was little. She was into them pretty big. Knew all the names. Her fave was the sort that grows in a big flat circle, green in the middle and all white and pink round the outside. Wreath flower, it's rare most years. You need decent rain. She was mad on it, said it was like an angel just landed there on the dirt. She said five minutes of mercy in this country and you've got a miracle on your hands. And I don't know if she's right but that's what wreath flower looks like when you find it next to a bush road out in bumfuck nowhere.

It's what I wanted on her coffin. But in February there's nothing to see but dry dirt and VB cans. Last summer there was no mercy and no miracles. Not any week or day of it. And when everyone went home after the funeral and I finished putting all them casseroles in the freezer I stood in the lounge in me good duds and the Captain sat out on the back patio drinking homebrew and rum. Arm over arm. Neither one of us said nothing. We both knew there was never gunna be anything good again.

I shoulda been making proper plans to go right then. But I wasn't. You ever seen a chased rabbit give in running? When he just pulls up and stands there? Like he's out of puff and out of ideas and can't put two moves together anymore? Well that was me. I shoulda been gone already. Shoulda been emailing

Lee, making arrangements. Christ, we coulda been on a bus to Marble Bar by then. It was like I was paralyzed.

Next day I spat a tooth up in the trough at work. Half a tooth really. And that look on his one-eyed face, that smile said it all. Like, what you gunna do now, mummy's boy, where you gunna go? Fucking nowhere. Because you haven't got the scrote to go.

That's what I mean about the nasty shit. The way it gets me off track from thinking something nice. Start out thinking of Lee and I end up on that stuff. Which is why I did so much shouting out there. Yelled till it burnt. That was me, gobbing off at trees like a loony.

The shadows got long. And the ground got a bit more stony. The dirt was pink now, red in patches, and soon big gum trees showed up. York gums that drop their bark from halfway up the trunk. Big gnarly buggers some of them. Standing round like old blokes with their shirts off. Scars and divits, man boobs and everything. Kind of funny to look at. Least when you're bone dry and half off your head from walking and yelling all day.

I kept on till it was nearly dark and then I come to a nice red dirt clearing and give it away for the day. Scuffed up some bark and sticks and got a fire going. Took me boots off. Scraped a clean spot to lay in.

The fire was decent. There was heaps of wood all round, dead stuff, grey and papery from white ants and it burned beautiful. And that was something at least.

That night I et the tin of pineapple. I was arse over tired

and really thought I'd go out like a light soon as I put me head down but I couldn't get off.

I wished I had a bottle of rum right then. And I don't even rate the stuff. Took pills a few times, that's more my thing. Only because I could jack them from Mum. It's like a fog comes on you. It's nice.

I musta been desperate. Wishing for rum I mean. Honestly, sometimes you'd rather be a dog. A mutt doesn't torture itself with thinking. Just licks its knob and goes to sleep. And that makes sense to me. Keeps a dog's life bearable, doesn't it?

Fact is I've met dogs smarter than the man my mother married. And I've had a long time to wonder how he got like he was. Maybe he was born like that. But, do people start out vicious? I fucking hate that idea. And I guess he had his worries, the Cap. But don't get me wrong, I hated the cunt. Nasty prick he was. And dead stupid. Who else could take their own eye out with a flyswat? Who else'd leave a breadknife half off the sink, handle out? Like the diving board at the pool it was. I'm standing there watching him chase this blowfly round the kitchen and it lands on the handle, right on the end. And wham. Next thing he's got the blade sticking out the front of his head. I was too bloody scared to laugh. But talk about funny. Mum comes in, goes Oh Sidney. He just chucks her against the piano and goes out and gets in the car. She lays there bawling till dark. And two days later he comes back from Geraldton with no eye.

Look, I'm not making excuses but maybe he knew what a piece of shit he was. Could be he was embarrassed of himself sometimes. I know he was frightened. When Mum got crook he was bloody useless. Had that panicked look like a ram all fucked up in barbwire. And once she was really bad he wasn't even there half the time. I thought that'd be a mercy, having him gone, sat out behind the shop all afternoon pouring it down with the copper, or passed out in the shed. But it wasn't better without him and that's the honest truth. No one should have to watch their mum die on their own.

But that's how it went down. Mostly them last weeks she sat in a chair by the window and said nothing. Like she was too weak or too sad to bother. But sometimes she perked up and got talking. About stuff she remembered. School. Picnics. Things she did when she was a bit of a lady. She never said nothing about Monkton. It was only the days before, happier times, like they were things she kept in a box locked away all these years. At the end she could only whisper and her stories got jumbled up to hell. And she went on about the same three things. This big New Year's party on the beach we went to. So lovely, so romantic. A concert too, Kasey Chambers it was, in Moora. And some rodeo at Mogumber. But I wasn't at any of them, it was nothing to do with me. Jesus, I never even been to Mogumber. And I was never at any beach party ever. She was so crook by then she thought I was him, for fucksake. She must of really loved him. That fucktard.

But she tried her best. I'm not dissing her. She was a good mother to me.

Still. Those last weeks I used to wonder what she thought about leaving me alone. She knew she was dying and I spose it's not easy to get things straight in your head, but didn't she want me safe when she was gone?

She never said a thing about it but I reckon before Christmas she woulda had plans. She was well enough back then. She woulda teed it up, talked to Auntie Marg. Said when the day comes promise me you'll drive down and collect Jackson. Please Margie, don't leave him there. Promise me. Yes I'd bet money on that. Mum woulda made sure and got me out, I woulda gone to live with me cousins in Mount Magnet. Which wouldna been easy, not for any of us. Still, family's family, isn't it.

But after Christmas Day Auntie Marg wouldn't have me in a bare-arse fit. Never wants to see my filthy face again. And it was like Mum thought I deserved it.

Which was the biggest surprise of my life. It's a hard thing to know about your own mum. That she'd side against you. But I've had time to think about this now and maybe I shouldna been so shocked. Because it was that way all along and I just couldn't see it. But now everything's burnt off me. All that kid shit. See, here's the thing. All those years in Monkton, once it got real bad with the Cap, did she really have to stay? She always said it was for me, she couldn't just take off and get herself free, there was me to think about. And I believed her. But now I'm thinking why didn't she just take me with her? We coulda packed up the car and gone anywhere together. Made a new life, just the two of us. Was she too scared of what Wankbag might do, frightened he'd come and find us? Or maybe I wasn't worth the risk? Maybe she figured like everyone else that I was a scumbag. See, my mum couldn't make herself choose me. Three's a crowd. She picked him.

I know dogs are fed scraps. And they're flogged, true. So it's not always the best life but sometimes, I tell you, being a dog wouldn't be so bad.

Anyway fuck it. This shit's no surprise anymore, I'm over it. But that night it was still fresh and it went deep. I burned a lot of wood and saw a lot of stars.

I wasn't real sharp next morning. Slept till the sun was already up. For breakfast I peeled an orange. It tasted better than any orange I ever had. I should of et that juicy bugger nice and slow to enjoy it properly instead of gutsing it down like that. But I was hollow and thirsty as hell.

When I pissed it come out dark and stinky. I figured pretty soon I'd be shitting gravel like a sheep. I stood round in me bare feet a while. Then I sorted me stuff, kind of halfhearted or maybe half asleep still. The Igloo jug was nearly empty. Like hoisting a bucket of air. But the rifle was getting heavier. I was still tight in the legs and sore all over now. When I sat down to pull me socks on and lace me boots up the bad eye stung something horrible. It was hot and throbbing and I wished I had something cool to put on it. I've used rump steak and frozen peas, cold flannels, everything you can think of. On the bus home from school once I had a shiner like a squashed plum and I walked past a girl with an icecream. Just snatched that thing and shoved it straight on me face and sat up the back. Beautiful it was. That chick and her mates and every other kid on the bus were so pissed off, and not a single one of them game to say a thing. I just let that mess melt down my face like I didn't give a fuck. But all I had this morning was orange peel. It was right on the ground in front of me. There was nothing else to go with so I picked it up and stuck it on. Christ, you coulda heard me howling from Sydney Harbour. Banana skins aren't bad for a bung eye but you can take it from me, orange peel isn't the go.

One thing I can say about it, it woke me up. I pulled me pack on and got going there and then.

The sun was in my face. I was raggedy at the start but then I got a sorta rhythm. And for a while it was real peaceful. If you know what I mean. Quiet. Just footsteps. Until I didn't even hear them anymore. All I heard was birds. Peewees it was. And that's a sound you don't get sick of. Reminded me of school. Sitting outside the principal's office. As usual. Them little birds they're game as Ned Kelly, no shit. There was a couple would come right in off the quadrangle. Every time. Right in under the verandah there to the bench where I was always parked up. Come just about to my feet. Neither one much bigger than your hand. Sticking their chests out, making that noise to see me off or just see what I'd do. And just remembering that made me happy.

Mum said school mighta been different for me if I only give a damn. Maybe it was wasted on me like the teachers said. I didn't have any philosophy in me then, so I didn't know what to listen for. Most of it was pointless crap. Don't reckon I met a single wise person all the years I stayed but like I say, I wasn't paying close attention. And the thing is I miss it a bit. That's something I never thought I'd hear myself say. I didn't know what I was, what I could do. Except the lame things I did do. But shit was always being done to me, every single day, and sooner or later you figure you should be the one doing unto others. So by Year Four kids were scared of me. And I spose I liked that. By the time I got to Dally District High they thought I was a psycho. Which suited me fine.

I stopped going last November. A coupla times after that them truant dogs come looking for me. But pretty soon everyone in the district knew about Mum's cancer. So they didn't bother me much after that. Maybe the old man said something to the copper. Anyway I think the school was glad I was gone. I never did make it easy for the teachers. With me temper and whatnot. Me delinquent antics they called it.

Jaxie Horsemeat, that's the name they give me. Like it was dead funny. And I put a price on them words, made sure any cunt I heard calling me that paid for it dear. No discounts, no exceptions, no deposit, no return.

And look, I've et horse meat. It's not that bad. People in town they're too soft to even eat roo nowadays. Pretty soon they'll wind up vegetarians and then they'll really have something to whinge about. Might as well go back to being monkeys.

Just because your old man does something epic stupid doesn't mean you gotta wear that all your life. Not my fault the Cap was a space case. Mum said it was the cards done him in. Then she blamed the computer and the online gambling. Like he had nothing to do with it himself. Made me sick. Any time I flogged a kid it wasn't to defend the Captain. Fuck that. I was standing up for myself.

But the teachers got jack of it. They got this funny-farmer up from Perth one time. I thought it'd be a bloke in a white coat but it's a chick in a teeny dress and she wants to know do I like bashing kids' heads in. I said yes because I knew she'd get excited. When she blushed it went all the way down the front of her. She was nice enough but she didn't have a clue what it was like to have a whole town laughing at you. And anyway maybe I did just like busting kids' faces in. Specially ones that gobbed off. I liked how quiet they got when they were flat on their backs sucking for air. She asked me was I lonely, did I have trouble at home. Jesus, what a genius. I told her I was all good, right as rain, and she musta believed me because she never come back. After that they just give me more detention. And a few times they suspended me, exclusion they call it, but the detention was better. It was worth catching the bus to sit out under the verandah all day and look at the flagpole and watch them aggro little peewees. Safer than staying home, I'll give you the tip.

Primary school wasn't so bad, I had a mate then. Kenny Chen. His oldies had the Chinee next to the pub. He was little and four-eyed but smart. He had this sly sideways way of talking, like cracking a joke without a smile. Kenny was a bit sarcastic really. Kids said he thought he was better than everyone which was ridiculous. He was just this tiny riceburner, why would he think that?

Way I saw it, people were a bit shit to Kenny Chen. So I started hanging round him, being friendly. Offering him a kick-to-kick at lunchtime and whatnot. If anybody give him disrespect I'd punch them out with extreme prejudice. Man, for a while there he was untouchable. It was like he got taller and more Australian every day. But then he went a bit weird. Even I thought he was getting cocky. He started making himself scarce at recess, hanging in the library. If I saw him in the street he wouldn't see me back. I wondered if his oldies didn't approve of me. Or if he thought I was gay. Asians, you know, they're not cool with poofs. And there was a time at the oval when I tried to put me arm round him, friendly sorta thing, and he flinched away. Kind of ducked like I was gunna thump him. And that hurt me feelings a bit. So I kept me distance after that but I still looked out for him. I'm loyal, me, and not many people understand what that means. Once I'm in I'm all in. For good.

Anyway the Chens left town one day without a word. Dunno why. I wish Kenny coulda stayed. By high school we coulda been Horsemeat and Dogmeat. We coulda reigned supreme, running amuck like two loser superheroes. Instead of just me by meself.

When high school started I had to get the bus to Dally. It was like people knew me before I even showed up. Every numbnuts

in the district wanted to have a go, even the Abos and fuck, they
fight wild. I was never big but I was game. Thing is, there was
nothing anyone could do to me that Wankbag hadn't done ten
times before, so I wasn't scared of anybody. Any prick wanted a
blue I'd give it to him hot and hard and I wasn't waiting round
till he was ready. There was this one kid hung shit on me for a
week. Never to me face but I heard about it. Trent Bisley. Old
man was some big grain agent. One day I got him in the throat
as he come out the gym. Big as a man he was, whiskers on his
face. Took him two days to get his voice back.

But I wasn't always like that. And I wasn't what everyone
thought. The thing with the teacher's car come out all wrong.
And the business with the crossbow, that never even happened.
People love a story. I know I give the teachers hell, gobbing off
the way I did but I didn't do it from nastiness. That was mostly
just for fun. And secretly I reckon some of them were into it,
thought shit I said was funny. Once after the funeral they sent
the truant dogs round after me again. It was like they missed
me and wanted me back.

But I'll never be back. I don't even know why, but it's kind of
a shame. Weird to be thinking of school, traipsing through the
mulga like that. I guess because of them birds and how peaceful it was.

The sun climbed up and settled hot and hard on me head.
I pulled a tea towel out and tied it on like one of them jihadis

and that helped a bit. I coulda done with a camel to go with it. And a drum of water big as a bone bin. Because by noon the jug was dry.

But then I got truly lucky. Even if I didn't know it yet.

I dunno how far off the highway I was when I saw the track. Maybe ten kays, coulda been more. But I come up on it dead unexpected. I was bearing north again more or less, and there it was under me feet all of a sudden, not much of anything really, just a coupla ruts across me path but it was a bit of a shock. I stood there gawking left and right like I was waiting for a gap in the traffic but no car had come this way in a long time, that was for sure. The dirt was baked hard. No tyre marks at all.

I had to sit a minute to get me head straight. The state I was in. I was dry as a camel's cookie and starting to feel pretty ordinary. I didn't get some water today, tomorrow at a pinch, I was rooted entirely and forever.

So here was this choice to make. West would take me to

the highway, I still knew that much. Meant putting up the white flag and I couldn't do it. But I told meself, you're no use dead are you? East was the ruts headed inland and I thought, well someone's made this track because something's out there. Or they hope something's there. Maybe something used to be there once and it isn't anymore. People only come out here for a reason. To cut sandalwood or prospect for gold. I used to come up this way shooting goats with Wankbag. Not here exactly but north of here. And I knew people set up where water was close by or they brought it in with them. There might be a tank or a mill trough or even a miner's water truck parked down there somewhere. It was long odds but not impossible.

Thing is, I'm not the surrendering type. Which might just mean I'm stupid like kids at school said. Or stiffnecked like the principal told me. Anyway I'm looking up and down that track. It was the highway or the wildywoods. That was the decision. Between something that's real and something you hope is real. The water you know is actually chugging up and down that road in trucks and old people's caravans and the drink you hope to fuck will be out there at the end of these ruts. I was banking everything on this call and maybe I wasn't fully right in the head by then but I went east. Roll the dice, that's me.

The ground that way was no different. Only it got more stony either side of the track. Reminded me of country we used to camp in. To go prospecting and plug a few goats. We had a big old F-truck back then and a metal detector and Mum used to come out too. Up by Lake Balthazar. Those weekends they were mad for gold. Took turns with that gizmo all day and even made me one of my own out of fencewire so I could follow them round. I was still pretty little then. On the last day we'd shoot a nanny and dress it out and ice it up in the big chest on the back of the truck and take it home. Mum said you could taste the saltbush in the meat. Most times we camped under salmon gums at the top of the lake, Mum up on the flatbed of the effy and me and him in swags on the dirt. On a big moon it looked like that lake was full of water instead of dry salt. It looked like a different country that thing, a whole nother continent. Went as far as you could see, this empty white space. Like something you could step into and get swallowed up and never find your way back. We never went out there. The gold was deep in the bush and the hunting was only good up on the ridges. We just drove down for a look now and then because it was so freaky. We always set up in nice clearings with dark red dirt and plenty of fallen wood. And we always had a good fire. Grilled T-bones from the shop and made jaffles in the mornings. Mum used to look for emu eggs. She'd take them home and blow them and etch them up, Abo-style, and a coupla times tourists saw them in the shop and bought them.

It was happy days out there when it was the three of us. Best times I can remember. Then Mum stopped going with us. She said she didn't like the shooting. And I spose that's fair enough because when I got older and learnt to use a rifle properly we did more hunting than fossicking for gold. And there was that weekend she got sunburnt so bad the skin come off her shoulders like wet paper. After that it was just me and the Cap. In the end we didn't bother with the metal detector at all. Them days he had a .222 Remington. That was a centre-fire outfit with a decent scope. We bowled a few roos over with it but mostly it was goats we hunted.

I figured three more days hiking, maybe four, I could be up in that country. Hide out for a while. Till everything cooled off. News gets old pretty quick. Maybe in a few weeks the highway'd be safe again. That was my thinking. I didn't start out with a plan like that, I just took off blind. But ever since I left the highway the idea'd been creeping up on me. Like, who in the wide world was gunna think I'd hole up along Balthazar? Only ones mighta guessed it were dead.

The last time we went on one of them shooting weekends another bloke come along. Dude called Bill Cox. He had a boxy old Land Rover and a .303 and a Mauser sounded like a bloody elephant gun. He reckoned him and Wankbag was in the army together but I'm not so sure. Neither one of them looked like any kind of soldier to me, they was both fat and beardy, more like bikies than soldiers. The two of them got pissed by the fire soon as we got there. They talked shit till it got dark and then they slept late and did the same all next day. The only shooting they did was blasting cans and bottles and they didn't even get off their arses to do that. I really wanted to go off on me own to knock over a goat or two but I wasn't game, not with those two blasting off all that big-calibre ammo left and right. So it was a hell boring weekend. I sat in the effy all day reading the same three comics over and over and wishing the time would go faster. We never popped a single goat the whole time, and

I couldn't get home quick enough. When I asked Mum later about the soldier stuff she said they was both overseas together but that's all I could get out of her.

I never did take to Bill Cox. Next time I saw him he was pulled up outside the house with a trailer full of chiller boxes. I saw the Mauser and the three-o when the passenger door opened. Wankbag come out the shed with a chainsaw and a swag and chucked them in the back and give me a look. And then they were gone. Dense pricks.

I dunno whose bright idea it was but it was dark days for the shop. I figure no supplier was even answering his calls anymore. So off he goes on a jaunt to the station country with Bill Cox and a chainsaw. Comes home with half a tonne of steak. Yeah, that was always gunna work. I never knew if it was brumbies or drovers' nags they sawed up but I don't reckon it woulda made much difference to the Meat and Livestock people. Anyway it didn't take long for that little scam to go guts up. I dunno how Wankbag kept his licence. It was all over the district. And things were already getting crook at home but after that everything was truly in the toilet.

Maybe I was caught up remembering all this stuff or just half tapped from thirst cos I nearly went past the diggings without even copping on. It was there on me left and halfway behind me before I took it in. I stopped like I'd forgot something and couldn't remember what. Then I turned round like the oldest man alive and saw the mullock heaps and piles of rusty cans and the sun flashing off the tin roof. The day was just about done and I was pretty much done too for that matter. But I stood there blinking like a knucklehead for a bit before I could believe it was real.

A shack. With a tin chimney and the last shreds of a sun-rotted awning hanging down in front like a fringe. And up on a stand right next to it a real life, honest to God water tank.

I stood gawking so long anyone inside that place coulda painted a picture of me, made themselves a cuppa and called the cops, but once the penny dropped I was flat on the dirt and crawling. Like I was some kinda Call of Duty dude instead of a twisted off retard who couldn't see a prospecting camp when it's there in front of him.

Anyway I got meself to the foot of a big pile of dirt and saw it was digging spoil. All round there was bits of wire and rotten lumber and hunks of rusting iron and hills of slag and stones. There was no smoke at the chimney and no clothes on the drooping wire strung from props out front. No vehicle neither.

I pulled the glasses from the case round my neck and watched the whole setup for a long time. Saw the tomato bush sprouting next to the tank. The only thing that moved out there was the canvas shade. I watched and waited as much as I could stand to. I woulda called out but I didn't have the wind for it yet. In the end I thought screw it, I'm gasping here, so I got up and went in real careful. I had the Browning out and up like some kinda badarse but the truth is I didn't even have a round in it. That day I was too dry and fucked up to get anything right.

It was one of them shacks a bloke and his mates chuck together in stages. You could see the original square of corry-iron walls and roof, the clouts half out from strong wind or bad work. And down one side there was a kind of add-on with a strip of louvres, some of them bogged up with ply or sheets of azzie. Bunged onto that was a dunny you could smell from Adelaide. Had a flystrip door and a tin-funnel shitter and not much else from what I could see. Fucking reek.

The front door of the place was shut. I give a croak but there was no noise from inside. I was still bricking it then but I was mad for a drink too. I turned the handle and it wasn't locked. I pushed the door back, peered in. It was gloomy inside and it stank. I hoped to fuck I wasn't about to find some prospector dead in his bed with a face like a rat-eaten pavlova. But there was no one. And no bed neither. Just a wood stove and a cement trough, a chrome chair with no back on it, and a table made of milk crates and half a door. The dunny door by the smell of it.

I shrugged me load and dropped it right there. I went straight out to the tank and when I whacked it with me fist it give a long thick shiver so I knew I was in business. The brass handle was gone off the tap but there was a vise-grips rusted on the stem and that did the job good enough. Water pissed out on the sticky dirt. It looked fine to me but it coulda been brown and I woulda gone it. I got down next to the tomato bush and sucked it straight from the tap.

It didn't taste that bad. Couldn't get the stuff down fast enough. I made noises I'm glad nobody could hear. If you never been that thirsty you won't know what I'm talking about. But I tell you, I drank till it felt like there was water in me balls and legs and feet, till me belly was hard and me back hurt. And when I finally left off I couldn't hardly get up again.

Staggered back into the shack like a wino, tripped over me pack and pitched up against the stove. Saw the bunky shelf with the bent saucepan and the black skillet and the tin of snaggly forks. Pulled meself off the cement floor and stood up to look round. And that's when I really saw how lucky I'd got. Because along the shelf was a bone-handle butterknife. Not just an ordinary butterknife neither. Before I even picked it up I saw it had an edge on it. When I ran it down the hairs on my arm it was wicked sharp. Some dude musta been grinding that thing day and night since before I was born. Just to pass the time. Why else would you up and leave it? Whoever he was he saved my arse.

The water was one thing. It spared me, true. For the moment anyway. But having a blade meant I could stay alive long enough to rest and figure things out. A gun'll get you meat, no question, but with no knife you can't hardly get to it.

Jesus, I was so relieved I nearly got a cry on. I just sat on that wood stove and tried to keep me shit together. Then after a few minutes I got this urge to get clean so I stripped off and grabbed the saucepan and went back out to the tank and doused meself all over. I stood in the sun on the stony dirt and dried off, feeling a whole lot better, but when I went inside and got me dirty clothes back on I felt all floppy and worn out so I just layed down on the cement floor and rolled me camo jacket up for a pillow and went to sleep.

When I woke up I didn't know where I was. Bars of light poked in through a hundred nail holes in the tin and for a second it was like I'd come to in the bottom of a cage. But then I saw the door half open and there was the rifle up against the wall and the busted chair in front of the stove so I knew I was okay.

Outside the mullock heaps were golden and the shadows from the trees were spilled long and flat across the gravel. I walked out in me bare feet a minute. It was nice to be stopped, even if it was only a while. I took a piss in a scrape full of old cans and wire and nests of plastic rubbish and thought, fuck me, who else leaves a mess like a miner. I felt calm. I noticed there was scat here and there, some of it pretty fresh, and all round the tank stand there was scuffs and diggings and more roo shit. That give me a bit of a charge. Like maybe I'd be orright here, could be this'd work.

I went back in and pushed a shutter open and set it on its pole for fresh air and light. Then got me boots on and went out and got some wood. There was plenty laying round, dead mulga and old bits of jarrah with wonky nails still in them. When I had enough to get me through the night I busted off a leafy branch and swept the mouse shit out of the place best I could. It was only near the end I found the broom behind the door and figured I'd finish the job properly tomorrow.

I set a fire in the grate but didn't light it yet. I spilled out everything I had on the floor and lined it up. Opened a box of ammo. I popped the mag from the Browning and loaded it. I layed the rifle and the mag on the milk crate table and sat just inside the open door, perched on the chair with no back. I figured maybe the roos'd come in at dusk and if I played me cards right I'd have some fresh meat by dark.

But nothing come in from the bush at all. Those diggings were flat and still as a picture.

When it got too dark to see much anymore I lit the stove and ate me last orange. Afterwards I was still hungry. That's what happens when you start thinking about fresh meat. But I wasn't down about it, I knew there was animals out there. They were a bit suss right now but they wouldn't be able to resist the smell of that water. There was always tomorrow.

I sat up that night and fed the fire till I was out of wood. It wasn't cold but the fire was company. In the end I packed it in and put me head down.

I was pretty wrecked and still happy but I didn't sleep that good. At first it was the hard floor. Then I got the gripes. I thought it was hunger pains but it wasn't bloody hunger pains. I squirmed and rolled for a bit. I wasn't about to try that filthy reeking longdrop in the dark so I put me boots on while I still had time and when I couldn't put it off any longer I ran out under the stars and got on with it. Christ, talk about bubble and squeak. I was in and out half the night, shitting like a duck. First I was worried about going out too far and stumbling down a hole. Later I was just glad to make it out the door.

I had all night to wonder what it was. Sunstroke makes you puke, it doesn't give you the trots. And it couldna been anything I et because there wasn't hardly nothing to eat by then. So that only left the water. I never did think to check the tank before I started drinking. Coulda been anything floating in there, some dozy possum maybe, or a crow thought it was a swan. Whatever it was it went through me like a rifle rag. Come dawn me date was so hot you coulda lit a spark plug off of it.

So I didn't do much that first morning at the prospector's camp. Dozed a bit. And twitched like a dog dreaming. It was kind of a flat feeling after being so buzzed the day before.

In the afternoon I climbed up the tank stand and looked in but with no torch I couldn't really see nothing. I started boiling the water anyway. I was glad of that saucepan.

Me guts stayed grumbly till dark but the worst of the gripes was gone. And even though I was parched again I settled for teeny sips from the jug until I felt decent enough to get some wood in and kick dirt over all the places I'd shat. And believe me that was a lot of places.

Just before dark a roo showed up behind the diggings. He edged out from the shadows of the bush but didn't come in any further. I stepped in the doorway and got the Browning and levered a round in real quiet. But that bung eye was me sighting eye. I had to faff round a second or two to match the good one to the rifle scope and that's what cost me. It was all too quick. I saw him lift his head a bit, like he was sniffing the air and didn't fancy it. He could probably smell my doings everywhere. Big red fella he was, all shoulders and ears. Wily too, like he'd been round the block more than once. And I reckon he wasn't just smelling me neither, he could feel me there. He propped quivering half a moment then turned on his heel and cranked off behind them big piles of spoil. And that was that.

It was only that hungry evening I finally copped on to why Wankbag stopped hunting so much. Wasn't the horsemeat thing put him off. Wasn't even the shakes he got from being a pisshead. It was his eye. The right one, that was his sighting eye. So after his flyswat caper he was all cock about. It got up me a bit that it took so long for me to figure out. Because I fucking hate feeling stupid.

So anyway there I was. Just as empty as yesterday. Just as weak too. But at least I was still kicking. I had water, if only I remembered to boil it. And a roof over my head. I had the makings to stay alive. I'd rolled the dice and got lucky. From here on I just had to stay smart. Be patient. Hold me nerve.

That night by the fire I made meself a little billy from an old bean tin and a hank of fencewire. It was something to do, kept me mind off food. And I needed all the boiling cans I could find now. But by the time I got the wire handle twitched on I was nearly out to it. Sometimes when you put your head down at the end of the day you know you're so rooted you won't dream a thing. Too tired to worry, too far gone to even work up a nightmare. That's another five minutes of mercy there.

Second day there me bung eye wasn't so bad. Puffy still, but not so tight. Just after sun-up I dropped a bungarra the size of a bloke's arm. Cocky bugger too. He saw me and never moved a muscle. He give me that look like, you wanna piece of me? Well bloody oath I did, I wanted all of him. So I went in the shack and got the Browning and he was still there when I got back, sunning himself at the top of a slagheap. One second he's the king of the castle, next thing his head's hanging off a twig ten metres away. What do they say? Rooster Sunday, feather duster Monday. Now you might think a .243 is a bit rich for knocking lizards but by then I was gagging for a feed. I would of used a cannon if I had to. And licked him off the leaves.

Cooked that goanna on the coals like a blackfella. And I'll tell you now I've et plenty worse.

There's a sad feeling in a place people have just walked out of and left behind. Could be only me thinks shit like this. And you could probably say there's plenty houses feel just as sad with people still in them. God knows our place was one of them for sure. Maybe it was just that empty shack getting on me tits.

I never really been alone in a joint before. Not properly alone. Somehow it's more lonely than being on your own in the bush. Could be why I got thinking about our house. It was never anything special, just another fibro like all the others in the street. Only thing fancy in the place was Mum's piano. And I never did get why that piano was there. Never saw anyone play it. Not for real. Me little cousins liked to pound on it when they come down from Magnet but there wasn't a single time I can think of when someone got a proper tune out of it. If Mum ever played it I never heard her. She dusted it every week, kept a line of photos in frames along the top of it. One of her and him on a beach somewhere. Maybe it was that party she talked about. They both looked young and happy. Her hair was long and he had no beard at all. There was a shot of me when I was a baby. I don't look real pleased in that picture. I had the face of some fat old prick wants his lunch in a hurry.

There was one picture of Mum on her own. She's singing. Like she's in a choir or something, holding a card or a book in her hands, and her eyes are aimed up like she's singing at the roof or maybe the sky. I always liked that one best. Every week she'd fluff the doily and dust the top of the piano and Windex the glass fronts of the photos. Then she'd Mr Sheen the piano. And sometimes I'd catch her staring at it. Like when we were eating tea. She'd leave off the telly a sec and gaze at the piano and get a look on her like she'd just thought of someone she knew from long ago, someone dead. And then she'd stick her fork into a snag and go blank.

I think of that photo now and then. Mum with her eyes set

up like that. Looking at something high. See, I didn't know her much at all. With Lee I know everything. But it's not the same with your mum. She's there all the time but she's mostly invisible. It's only when she's gone you get that wanting feeling and get curious. Lee wants me to know her. I don't reckon Mum ever really did.

If anyone heard this shit they'd say I had too much time to think out there in bumfuck nowhere. And it's true I had more time to cogitate on things once I got clear of town and people and all that mess. Cogitate, that's a word I didn't even know back at the diggings but I like the sound of it. Bloke who taught it to me was full of words. Christ, he had so many he was drowning in them. He was someone did a lot of cogitating. Had time enough to do it. But he was a dude wanted you to know him. Even if he didn't really dare when it come down to it. Said it was too dangerous. And maybe it was. Me, I got nothing to lose. Not now. Only Lee.

After the bungarra I got nothing at all for two days. Not one thing come in round the shack and the diggings. So I spent the nights hungry again. I boiled water in me little tin billy and drank it hot because that way it feels like it takes up more space. If I'd seen a crow or a galah I'da shot and et either one. I could hear peewees out past the miners' crap but none come close. It was like the whole world out there was suss on me. Honest to God, I would of et anything, a snake, a grasshopper, a thorny devil. Any living thing that crawled by. But nothing did, not when I was looking. Thought about eating plain red dirt a couple of times but that's for crazy bastards at the end and I was a way off that yet. The best I could do them days was a few bushflies and they wasn't exactly swallowed on purpose. All that kept me going was hot water that tasted of smoke and beans and burnt tin.

Two other things I turned up round the shack was a hat and a map and it was really only the hat that was any use. Just an old black cap it was. Penrite Oil on the front. Dirty and chewed half through by moths, a piece of shit hat really, but it fitted good enough and it was better than going round like an Arab with a rag on his head.

The map looked like some bloke drew it to work something out for himself. And he didn't sketch it careful, just a rough outline of WA sawn off the rest of Australia. Monkton and Dally wasn't even on there. Not Lake Balthazar neither. Only Perth and Kalgoorlie and Broome and Halls Creek and Wyndham. And a few figures in a line to one side. PER–KAL 590, PER–EUCLA 1428, PER–WYNDHAM 3227. Looking at those faded numbers took the wind out of me. It's one thing knowing it's three hundred kays from Monkton to Magnet. But getting us ten times that far, that's something else. The map wasn't any use to me, it was just something to look at and pretty soon I figured I shouldn't look at it too often.

I mostly mooched round the diggings them days. You had to be careful because there was pits and holes and channels everywhere. I didn't wanna get this far and then fall down a mineshaft and snap me neck like a carrot. Or if the fall didn't take you out you could wake up down the bottom of a pit looking up at a little blue square of sky like one of them poor buggers in a movie. I woulda liked to check out some of them old shafts with timbered frames and iron ladders but the wood was soft and grey and the steps rusted half through so I wasn't game to try. Everything you saw and touched out there looked like tetanus waiting to bite your arse. Trenches full of jagged tins and broken glass, shotgun shells and rifle casings. There was piles of bottles taller than me, beer bottles, whisky bottles, Coke bottles, champagne bottles, shortneck stubbies and tiny fat medicine bottles, blue and green and red. It was like a museum full of redbacks and snakes. When I pulled up sheets of tin I found old boots and buckles, half a saddle some rat had bored right through. There was rusty bed frames with weeds growing up through them and rolls of wire that come to bits soon as you touched them. It was a bloody mess out there, like there'd been a war on and everyone had just packed it in, like suddenly they were fed up and fucked off. I wondered how many blokes ever got rich from it, how many even found enough gold to buy their mates a round at the pub.

Now I look back I can't believe what I was doing at the prospector's camp. It was good to have somewhere to meself but I was sitting round starving to death. I wasn't hunting food, not seriously. It was like I was too scared to go far from the water and the roof over me head.

It was out in them junkpiles I found a toasting rack made of fencewire. A good one too, one you could flip the bread in and keep holding over the coals of a fire. But all it did was make me think of bread.

And I thought about spuds a lot. The way we used to have them of a Sunday. Roasted in fat with salt all over them.

Thought of fried eggs and bacon.

Thought of rissoles and tomato sauce.

And bananas.

And cold milk.

None of that thinking was any use at all.

I got dozy enough to sit in the shade one day and spark the phone up. It said No Service but I pulled up Lee's number anyway and looked at her face. It was an old photo, one I took at the rez. Just her in that gay hat she found. She looks different now. And even if there was some coverage out there it was no use calling because it'd be Auntie Marg picking up, not Lee. I wasn't softheaded enough to forget that.

And then I spose I wised up before I wasted away to nothing. I got off me freckle, geared up and pushed out into the bush. It was hard leaving the shack behind. Once it was out of sight I got a flutter. I was ashamed of meself but I couldn't help it. I kept me bearings and left markers and tried to concentrate on the job of getting meat.

I was only gone a few hours but it was a rough run. I was almost back at the diggings and out of juice before I saw anything worth a shot. A little euro come bouncing in through the gimlets like he didn't have a care in the world. Which he didn't till I showed up. There's no other kind of roo pretty as a euro. You could see he wasn't expecting anyone. Reckon he never seen a human in his life before. He pulled up just as I got a round up the spout and that's when he saw me proper. He looked more curious than scared. I'm trying to get me breath under control, keep him in the scope, and he's wondering what the deal is. One ear my way, the other twitching round. I told meself not to rush it, I had plenty of time. But hell, I was hungry enough to eat leaves by then. I couldn't afford to miss.

That euro figured out pretty quick there was something wrong about me. So he made that first turn sideways like it was time to bust a move. Then he pulled himself forward a bit, the way they do. Glanced off to the south. And I knew for sure he was ready to bolt. He looked my way one more time like he couldn't help himself and as he turned his head back to go I had him.

For half a sec, before the sound of the shot caught up, it was just like his neck had an itch. Then he went down on his arse as the sound let out like a hard slap. You always know when you've hit something. Even if you blink and don't see it go down. It's a thump you can't mistake. You can hardly believe a bit of lead the size of your pinky nail can make a noise like that and do that kind of damage. It was beautiful.

I tell you I was glad to be so close to camp when I took him down. He was only small but I don't think I'da been able to haul him in from any further out. Once I made it back and got a fire lit on the ground out front of the shack I found that butterknife wasn't the best bit of butchering gear you'll ever use, but it done the job good enough. By the time I had that fella skun and hung from a tree I was red to the elbow. Blood gloves is what it looked like, and when the gore went dry and tight on me arms it felt like gloves too.

I didn't want dingoes and feral cats coming round for the skin and guts, so I wrapped it all together and walked it out to one of them deep shafts and dumped it in. Then I washed off at the tank with a bit of sand and water. I wondered if I'd still be there when the tomatoes come good. I wondered what I woulda done if I'd missed that euro. But that was like wondering what your life'd be like if your dad wasn't a douche.

I was ready to eat, I'll tell you that for free. I couldn't even wait for the fire to die down so I could cook that poor little bugger. Before he was even properly bled out I cored a loin out of him and I don't mind saying I et it raw. Then I ripped some more cuts off and layed them on the fridge rack I'd scabbed from the miners' junk and watched them fizz and twist over the coals. It was meat tasted like nothing you ever had in your life.

That night the stars come out early and clear as I'd ever seen them and I could smell everything in the bush round me. I tasted smoke and gum sap in the air. Moths and bugs heavy as birds bumped and skidded off me. It was like my blood was bubbling, like food had charged me up fresh and new. I was knackered but I knew I wouldn't sleep. I was too excited, so relieved. I just piled wood on the fire and watched the Milky Way running down the sky like spilt fat, and next thing I knew the birds was stirring and I'm out there on the dirt next to a warm pile of ash.

There's one thing I learnt being out that way. There's more meat on a spring lamb than a euro. After breakfast there was hardly enough left to take with me for lunch.

I went further that day, out into country full of desert pines and yorkies. And I took down a grey big enough I had to field dress it and heave it home on my back. I could of done with that Ka-Bar knife back in the safe. And a gambrel too. It's no fun butchering a roo in the dirt. But I come in with more meat than I could eat, more than I could properly keep. I was too tired that night to see the problem, too glad of the food and the place to come home to.

I strung that doe up from a dead tree by one of them piles of junk. There was rope out there and no shortage of wire. I wished I had a gambrel again but I made do and ripped him best I could and grilled big chunks and stuffed me face.

That night I slept inside on the hard cement floor and I tell you, it coulda been a waterbed. All night I dreamt I was out at the train tracks behind the house. There was no one home. Only the washing turning on the line in the wind like a white wheel behind me. I just walked on down the tracks. And when the first wheat train come rumbling in across the paddocks I didn't step off, I walked on through it. I could smell the diesel and the orange peel on the floor beneath the driver. I could taste the steel of the cars and the grain dust that hung in the air after it was gone. It was like I couldn't be stopped. I was gunna keep walking till I got where I was going. But I couldn't remember where I was headed. That was the thing of it. And I went through it over and again like something stuck.

I et pretty hard for two days. Went at that grey roo like a bull shark. At first because I was hungry and then because I had to. Bits of the carcase were on the turn by the end of the second day. The tree where I had it strung up was mad with ants and flies and the crows got into it soon enough. The only thing I could do to keep it good a little longer was get the juice out of it. That meant cooking what was left. So that's what I did. Hacked the haunches off and roasted them. Sounds easier than it was. It was always gunna take too long to bone it out with that butterknife so I left the legs whole. Didn't have a bone saw of course. Used a rusty iron bar to bust the shins. Wasn't pretty but it done the job. Then I folded them all up and shoved them in the oven. Stoked the stove till the shack was too hot to sit in. Cooked that meat till it was hard and dry as a publican's heart. It was brutal to cut and a bastard to chew. But beggars can't be choosers.

And I guess by then I could see how things really were. I had two boxes of shells and one of them I'd dipped into already. If I wanted to last out there more than a week or two I had to make every shot count. You can't hunt every day and waste half of what you get. And I didn't want to leave so much spoiled meat out there I'd have wild dogs coming round. What I needed was some way to keep meat. There was nothing I had to keep it cool. I figured smoking might work, but the Cap never got round to showing me how to do it. Only other thing I could think to use was salt, but I didn't have any of that neither.

And that's the joke of it. Because there was a billion tonnes of salt close by.

I can't believe how long it took me to cop on. When it finally come to me I was looking at that pissy map. And Lake Balthazar wasn't even on it.

Next morning I was up and fed in the dark because I didn't really know how long the hike was gunna take. I was hoping to be back before sundown. Thought if I followed them wheel ruts I'd hit the saltpan sooner or later, come home with a packload, enough to get by on for a while. I was fully rolling the dice again but I didn't even know it then because I was so fixed on the idea, banking everything on the salt being as close as I figured. It was a bigger punt than I knew and if it hadn't of paid off the way it did, which wasn't anything like the way I expected, you'd be coming across my bones in fifty years' time wondering who this poor fella was pegged out in the middle of nowhere. So don't ever feel sorry for Jaxie Clackton. Because I'm one lucky bastard, I kid you not. Or maybe it's like Fintan said. I was sent. I'm destined. Be dead five times over if I wasn't. Wouldn't be where I am today, three hours away from everything that matters in the world.

So I was all business that morning. Been scheming half the night. And by first light when I come out that door I had a full jug of water and plenty of meat in me pack. I had the glasses strung off me neck and the .243 over one shoulder. Me mind was already on the track east. I wasn't ready for company. So when I saw someone standing out in the gloomy grey by the slagheaps I nearly shit meself. Took two seconds to see it wasn't a man at all, just a big old roo the size of a fullback. He stood up straight and hitched his elbows and I don't even know why I shot him except he was there. Can't even say how I got the drop on him so quick. He sat back on his tail and fell sideways and I thought fuck me, now what.

I didn't have time to dress him out properly so I just strung him up, fetched his guts out and ditched them down a shaft. He was as big of a roo as I ever got close to. Rusty red. And heavy. I left the hide on. And the head. Which wasn't ideal but I had to get going. Figure it out later.

I guess it's a rotten thing to do, bowl a roo over and just leave him there. But I didn't know I'd be gone so long. And it's hard to turn down a feed when it's standing right in front of you.

By the time I hit the track the sun was up and I was covered in blood. When I got past the diggings I looked back and it wasn't a real pretty scene to see. All that dug up and fucked over ground. The sadsack humpy in the middle of it all. And out the front, hanging from a gum tree, a body twisting in the wind like some poor bastard's had enough of this prospecting caper and strung himself up to be done with it.

That was the last time I saw the place.

The wheel ruts were no trouble to follow. There was no breeze, it was coolish still and decent walking. I hustled on quick as I could without blowing a flange. The little tin billy was the only noise I heard. I had it hung off the pack and it give a rattle and squeak nearly every step I took.

Far as I could tell I was about a week gone from Monkton. Lee would of heard about everything by now. She'd be wondering where I was, why it was taking me so long. Then she'd figure it out. She's smart, Lee. And she knows me well enough. In her wardrobe she'd have a bag ready. She'd wait. However long it took me, she'd wait. I just had to hope Auntie Marg hadn't sent her off to boarding school in Moora. Or Perth, that'd be even worse. But that woulda only happened if she played up, if she carried on like a pork chop instead of sucking it up and staying chill. She'd keep smart and act like someone not waiting at all. She'd still be there in Magnet. I couldn't of kept going if I thought she wasn't.

Middle of the morning the track come round northwards and I saw the first rocky ridge sloping down west to east. So I stopped for a bit of a breather and a sip. And in the quiet I heard a bird I always like, one with a sad song that gets me every time. Butcherbird. How fucked up is that?

I got off my arse again and set out for the ridge. But it was further away than it looked. By the time I got to the foot of it the sun was overhead. The track got pretty rugged up that hill. There was washouts knee-deep some places. I figured no regular car would stand a chance and even with a 4×4 you'd have a job on your hands getting through. High up, the scrub was just thorny stuff et down to stubs by goats and their shit was everywhere. The rocks were red and yellow with chunks of quartz like frozen milk.

When I got to the top I looked north and saw another jump-up maybe two kays off. It was higher and stonier by the looks. The valley between that and the one I was on was blue with trees and shadows. To the right it tipped down like I hoped it would and there in the east, across all them treetops, was the shiny pink-white skin of the lake. It was far enough away I knew right then I wouldn't get back tonight but seeing that salt give me a bit of a charge so I didn't crack sad about it.

But it's true I stopped there a bit, sucking it up before I started along the spur. I couldn't help looking. It was a good thing I had the wheel ruts to follow because without them it'd be hard to find me way back.

I took the down slope careful and come into the valley where everything was cool and shadowy and the salmon gums were shivering with birds. The going was easier here and I reckon most people'd say it was beautiful in the valley with all them million trunks and branches, prettier than the mulga I been in all this time, but you couldn't see far ahead and it was a bastard picking real from shadow, so I wasn't really getting off on it. And like I said, the hiking was good but there seemed no end to that valley.

We always got along good, me and Lee. She's younger by six months, I'm July 2 and she's the fourth of December. And I spose we got to be mates because sometimes we were all we had for friends. If Auntie Marg wasn't down at ours we was up there at Magnet. Long weekends, school holidays. One time we all went in caravans to Coral Bay, back when me Uncle Ted was still round. And there was a summer we got a beach shack at Dongara, all of us crowded in together, it was sick fun. We did everything together, all the kids, all the grownups. But I spose the women and the children was the closest. There's something about the men just stops them being able. Anyway Uncle Ted done a flit when Lee was ten. Woulda been better if the same thing happened to Mum. You ask me, it's safer when they shoot through.

So we grew up together, me and Lee. For a long time she was the only girl I really knew. Up close that is. We used to go out scooping taddies and stuff. Dink each other on our bikes. I liked it when she was round and when she wasn't I sort of missed her. Maybe that's why I didn't care so much about kids at school. Because there was always Lee.

I didn't even know why I liked her. She was just there. I was used to her. Like I said, we did stuff together. The others were just babies. I remember when she lost her front teeth. She couldn't even say my name right. She chased me across the oval calling out Jackthee! Jackthee! I'll git you Jackthee Clackton! Sounded like a retard. I couldn't hardly run for laughing.

Thing is, she wasn't like girls from school. She was game. And she wasn't a whinger. She wasn't one of them girls always fussing and farting about her dress or her shiny little shoes or getting her knees dirty and whatnot. She could throw a ball for one thing. But mostly it was that she was up for doing shit. Fun stuff. When Susie and that little sook Norman was plonked down watching *The Lion King* over and over we'd piss off up the granites or out the rez. That's if we was in Monkton. Up at Magnet we'd go to the pool but I liked it better at the granites or out the rail line where there was no one else to deal with.

In summer the granites was always too hot so mostly it was the rez. That's just a kind of big stone tank they built in the old days for watering the trains. There's huge flat rocks you can jump off or lay round on. If you dive deep enough it goes all cold and green and it's so slimy and gross on the bottom you can hardly let yourself touch it.

At the granites there's gnamma holes the blackfellas stored water in when it rained. Some of them's only big as the inside of a hat. Lee and me used to get taddies up there and find bones in caves. Bird bones or bits of bandicoots or something. They wasn't real caves, just bits that hung over, or long cracks in the side you could wiggle into and get cool. I liked the feel of the lichen stuff growing up the walls. On the far side there's steep bits like cliffs you can monkey up barefoot if you're game. That was a thing when we were little. Lee could get up a steep rock like a rat up a drainpipe. Later on when we got older we mostly just layed round in the sun there. Talking I spose. Or not talking at all, which was just as good.

When we get out of Magnet we'll have plenty of time to do either one, talk or not talk. It's a lot of road to cover, all the way north. In Darwin we can work on a prawn trawler or head east for Queensland.

Lee's got one eye green and the other grey. Makes her sound freaky but it's not like that at all. Her hair's thick and straight and wheaty coloured. When she was little her mum used to curl it. Made her look like a bloody spastic. And maybe that's why she snuck off and got it cut short like a boy last year. Can't say I liked it at first. But I got used to it. When you run your hand over her head she felt like a puppy. But that was before everything went to shit. And now she's got hardly no hair at all.

It was nice hiking that valley. The old wheel ruts were pretty faint in places but the track wasn't that hard to follow. It snaked about a bit, winding downhill all the way, the slope so gentle you mostly didn't notice it. And everything round was cool and cut up with shadows. The ground was gravelly, or gritty more like, but covered over here and there with dead sticks and dry leaves. Salmon gums all bunched up like that, they make hard country look pretty. Cockies and twenty-eights flew past in mobs. I saw quail and plenty of birds I didn't know at all. I coulda shot enough meat to feed meself for a week. Euros mostly, and an emu or two. I was happy just being there. Close to where I was headed. Keeping up a good speed. And kinda lost in my thoughts.

Lee got grounded from Christmas to New Year's. Worse than grounded, she was locked in. Boxing Day she cut all her hair off with dog clippers. All of it, like fully number one. And when she messaged me to let me know I couldn't believe it, I thought she was bullshitting me. Then she sent a picture. And fuck, it was terrible. Her eyes were huge and sad and them shears musta been rough as guts cos she had cuts all over her. She was like something I seen in a movie, a girl getting ready to be burnt at the stake. It bloody frightened me. But she said it made her feel strong and pure. After a while I guess I got that, I think I understood, and pretty soon her picture put some steel in me. Still does. That's when I knew we'd outlast all them cunts, every one of them. It was like she did it for both of us. So I buzzed my head too. Then I totally shaved it. And Christ, Mum really did her nana. Then she bawled her eyes out. Wankbag knocked me down the front steps and said I was a fucking disgrace, didn't I have any fucking feelings for my mother. It was only then I remembered. Mum was wearing a wig most of last year. I guess it give them both a fright seeing me with a bald head. But I wasn't thinking about any of that when I done it. I didn't do it to be a smartarse. She stood and watched him flog me right in the street. After that I didn't give a shit what either of them thought.

For the longest time I didn't know there was anything special with Lee and me. Anything more than being mates. I didn't know about that kind of stuff, not till we was about eleven. It was one time up the rez when things got strange. That day it felt like everyone in town was up there. Those high school kids were making a big circus show of themselves. You know, rolling durries and talking loud and chucking each other in, and after a while the smaller kids got up and left and it was just us and the teenagers, and every time they laughed it was like the joke was on us. It was kind of miserable but we didn't want to go home, so we just sat there on the shady side and didn't swim or nothing. We camped on our towels and tried to make ourselves invisible and talked shit back at those kids in whispers so they couldn't hear. I didn't want a blue that day but I knew if one of them come over and said something straight out at us I woulda had to go him there and then. And maybe I would of got me block knocked off but whichever prick did it woulda took a few for his trouble. Lee reckons I'm all bite and no bark but I'm way chattier now than I used to be. Funny how talky you get when there's no one round to listen.

Anyway it got hot about lunchtime and soon them high school kids packed it in and it was just us at the rez. And the shade was gone from the rocks our side so we chucked off our shirts and shorts and went in like we'd been let out of prison.

The water was brass monkeys. We mucked round splashing and that and she did this big lap up and back, showing off her freestyle cos she's the kickarse swimmer in the family. Magnet school champion Auntie Marg reckons, though I never seen a trophy. After a few minutes we're both shivering like rabbits. And just by the step rock that's all slimy and weedy and makes you think twice about climbing out we kinda bumped together, each trying to be first up. It was a deadset accident, something you wouldna thought nothing of. I just bumped into the back of her and she turned and looked at me and put her arms round me and then we were hugging. Hugging against the cold pretty much and then holding on hard, pressed up bone to bone. And it was funny. We started laughing. Until I got a horn on. Then she got out and I swum round till it was safe and we both pretended everything was normal.

Afterwards we was just layed there in the sun warming up, kind of shy, but I couldn't stop looking at her. Her hair pushed back and dripping on the rock and her hand over her face for shade and her skin all goosey from the cold. Bikinis she had on. Them brown arms and legs. And the look of her there on the rocks was like a kick in the guts. After that I guess it was never really the same for the both of us.

But nothing happened. Nothing we wouldn't normally do. Not for a long time anyway. We was just kids, we did kid stuff. And we didn't have things to do like people in the city. We couldn't catch the bus to the beach or the movies or hang out in big shopping malls. We had to ride everywhere or shanks it. Go for a milkshake at the roadhouse, check out the tip. Because there was no KFC or Subway. We'd walk along the highway looking for eagle feathers. She's fully into animals, Lee. She comes up with shit about birds and snakes even I don't know. She says sometimes I'm a bull looking for a china shop but when she's round I don't feel like that. There's people might say she talks too much but it doesn't bother me. In our house no one hardly said a word. Jesus, it's nice to hear someone talk.

Before we got our own phones Lee used to ring me from the landline at Magnet or I'd skate up to the public phone outside the roadhouse. Once or twice I called her from the shop. And we just talked shit really, like anyone else. If it wasn't about animals it was people we knew or wished we knew or people who were hell famous. And we liked to muck round. What would Ryan Gosling look like with JLo's head, that sorta thing. It didn't need to be anything important. I was just happy when I heard her voice, the sound of her laughing. Deep down I did remember that feeling from the rez though. And I wanted more days like that. Once you been up close and hard like that with someone it's tough to forget.

I only ever got the shits with Lee the one time. We never had fights. All our arguments were for fun, just taking the piss. But I didn't like it the time she said I walked funny. It was out by the silos she said it. And then she did my walk, right in front of me, and it got me wild. I could see it straight away when she did it along the gravel road. I recognized it. But I was fucked off. Fully. I didn't hit her or nothing, didn't even tell her to take it back. I just left her there. Walked away. With me hands in me fucking pockets. And later at the oval she said she was sorry. And I asked why she'd do something like that. And she said because she understood me. She got me and she wanted to show me she did. She said I had this elbows-out walk like a scorpion all burred up for a fight, so it made me look bigger. And I could of punched her in the throat then because I don't like people laughing that I'm small. She said it was natural, that puff adders did it and blowfish too. But I didn't need to do it round her, was all she was saying. So it turned out she wasn't sorry at all. And I told her that, kind of hot and raw, and she admitted it was true. And it's funny but I stopped being wild at her then. The steam just went away. Maybe I saw what she meant. Like I could relax with her. Lee's the only one I don't have to worry about trying shit on. She's the only person doesn't want to fight me, cut me down.

And you know someone's special when you never get enough of them.

After Auntie Marg lost the house Lee and the others come down every holiday and lots of weekends. We never went up to Magnet much anymore. Mum said it was because they had to move into the pub where Auntie Marg works and she was embarrassed. Anyway having them down was cool. Lee and me didn't waste a single minute. Them coupla years things got hectic. But there was always family everywhere, beds and bodies in every room, nowhere to be alone. So from breakfast to dark we just pissed off together and did our own stuff.

Sometimes we rode out past the silos to that patch of salmon gums on the edge of town. And there was the grandstand if no drunks were about. In winter we got on the roof of the old bowls club and that was mint. No one goes out there, the greens are all dead and there's been no one playing for years. We layed up there on the asbestos till our backs got rippled, it was just us and the black cockatoos. Then I guess it went where it always goes. Don't need a diagram to explain that, I reckon. We're just two ordinary people.

And okay, she's me cousin. Mum's sister's daughter. There's bugger all we can do about that. We didn't ask to be cousins. We didn't ask to be born. And we didn't plan on this. One thing Mum told me, love isn't always convenient. Well she got that right. Even if she pretended later she never said it at all.

This thing just snuck up on us. You might think we're dirty bastards and too young to be at this sorta thing but actually I don't give a shit what anyone thinks anymore. I'm sick of getting the piss kicked out of me, tired of cunts looking down their nose like I'm nothing. This is what I got, it's all I got. It's better than anything I ever had before and I'm not saying sorry for it and I'm not backing off, not for anybody.

You probably just think it's about rooting. Yeah, whatever. You can say what you like, whatever gives you a tingle. But that isn't even the half of it. Not like we were at it all day. How could we be? In Monkton or Magnet, places so small everyone's watching? You wouldn't understand if you never had to buy frangers off truck drivers. You can't be walking into a shop asking for a pack of condoms unless you want everyone in town to know what you're up to. You're always on the lookout, sneaking and creeping about, grabbing your chances. Everything's gotta be squared away and normal looking. The biggest thing in your life and it's deadly secret.

And that eats at you. Even the buzz of hiding it wears you down. Best we could do was imagine everything being different. Sometimes we'd be squished in some crack at the granites or even just riding up and down by the silos and all we'd be doing was this daydreamy thing about having somewhere we could go. A house of our own. Or one of them Winnebagos tourists had. Maybe one day we could slip up the back stairs of the Railway, find ourselves a room that was empty. A bed and a sink and a tall window with the blind down. All to ourselves. Just to lay there on pillows and sheets with the door locked. When all you get is dead grass and asbestos roofs and the stinky shade of the grandstand, the idea of a proper room is deadset luxury. It was a fun thing to talk about, making this picture up together. Being right with each other. Left alone.

Neither one of us ever really said so out aloud but both of us knew we'd never be safe and happy the way things were. Being secret is cool, but I don't reckon it's as good as feeling decent and safe. When you get talking about a room to yourselves and cooking up scenes of how it could be, like something off TV, you know there's no chance for you at home. Lee and me were always gunna have to get away. We just never got to make a plan. How things were made us careless as well as crazy.

Some days you hoof along with your head full of memories and you've been so took up with thinking you can't hardly believe how far you come, like you arrive just after you started. Well that day in the salmon gums it wasn't anything similar at all. God knows, me mind was busy but the track just went on and on like someone was up ahead out of sight making it as he went and some other prick was growing new trees and birds either side all ready for me, just to keep the joke going and piss me off to the living fuck.

I swear I got thinking that valley was gunna go on forever.

Then it got so late I packed it in. Made a fire and kicked me boots off. I had a brew and a decent feed of cold meat but I can't lie about it, that night I dropped me lip a bit. And I never slept much neither. Bloody trees cracked and whispered and farted and groaned all night.

I started out next day feeling pretty ordinary. Didn't think much. I was just looking for a break in the trees, a bit of white to get me hopes back up.

It was after bloody midday when I finally come out in the open. A while before that the trees got a shine behind them like they was thinning out, but it wasn't that so much as eventually there was no more trees past them, nothing at all but stumpy saltbush and samphire. I spose I wasted a lot of time at the shore just staring at it, trying to take it in. The salt was more blotchy-looking than I remembered. And the lake was bigger than you could get your head round.

The wheel ruts I was following took a turn north but you could see plain as a donkey's donger no one had driven down here lately. At the bend there was two deep trenches where someone musta got himself bogged to the living shithouse but now the mud was all baked hard again.

I stepped off the track about there. I had no use for it any-more. Went on through the samphire till it thinned out to nothing but salt. It was strange going, flat to look at but uneven to walk on. Mostly it was packed hard but now and then one boot sank a little and then you didn't know what to expect. It was like you didn't know if you could trust what you were look-ing at and sometimes it was hard to keep me balance with all that gear hung off me.

I pulled up after a while and got down to scrape up a half a handful. But the salt here was dirty-looking with bits of black stone through it. The softest patches had kind of grey veins in it like something gone off. So I kept on.

Maybe a hundred metres out I come to a dip I didn't even see until I stumbled into it. Everything was so bright and glary it all looked even, but the ground sunk gradually into a crater no bigger than a farm dam and in the middle of that it got so soft you went right through the crust and up to your ankles. Once you broke through the white icing it was all purply mullock underneath and in the end I was using the rifle like a walking stick to get through. Man, that stuff stuck like shit to a blanket.

By the time I got across to the good white pan on the other side me boots was just two huge blocks of stinking goo and as it come off in dags and splats you could see the trail of it plain as day behind. But even on the better stuff I left footprints that'd give me away and I didn't like the feel of that.

I got out far enough that the trees were like a greeny blue strip behind me and past that the ridge had the sun nearly on it already. Looking east you could just make out the other shore.

But left and right the lake went on as far as you could see.

I plugged ahead and when the salt looked dry and clean enough I shrugged all me stuff off, took a quick sip from the jug and layed out the two tea towels I brung from home. The one from under me hat was pretty manky now but I couldn't afford to get particular. If I'd been that particular I woulda had a spare shirt or some clean undies but I never brung neither one. Still, I was glad I had something to scrape that salt onto. I used the cup from the waterjug, scratched away till I had a pile I could mash up into a ball the size of a pig melon or maybe a baby's head. Then I screwed each towel off and twitched it with a bit of rusty wire. After that I just shovelled cupfuls of salt straight into the pack, deep as my hand, and then I set those two parcels down into it where they wouldn't spill. But that shit's heavier than you think. When I got the pack snibbed up again it felt like it was loaded with rocks.

I don't know how much time all this faffing about took. Turned out getting salt off the lake wasn't as quick and easy as I thought. Wasn't hours or nothing but it was long enough I started to get a bad feeling. I already knew I'd be camping in the salmon gums again tonight. And that roo wasn't getting any fresher hung off a tree the way it was. But it wasn't that giving me the yips. It was being this far out in the open and taking so long to get the job done. Hell, by now anyone within a country mile coulda seen me on that big bare pan. And it was like I was starting to see things.

I got the pack hooked on and brushed me hands clean. Then I reached down for the rifle and the waterjug and when I stood up straight I had this dark patch bobbing at the edge of me good eye. You been whacked in the head as many times as me, you get used to floaty spots and stars. Sometimes it's just an eyelash but not this time. It was a black splotch. In all that white. I turned me head away, it was gone. Looked back, it was there. Up north a way. Dancing in the warm wavy light.

Aw fuck me, I said out aloud. Snatched up the glasses from round me neck. Saw it was something dark and thin and tall. Or someone. I couldn't be sure. But it sure looked like someone. I couldn't guess the distance. Couldn't pick a face neither. I let the binoculars drop and broke into a run.

There was no shout. No shot yet. And once I was running I couldn't see much at all.

I tried to go round the mucky patch but got caught up at the edges. Nearly went arse over. By the time I was through the samphire and into the first line of trees I was really blowing. Dropped flat and looked back through the rifle scope and couldn't figure how I hadn't noticed before. It wasn't just one of them out there. I counted three now. No, four. All pulled up in a bunch. Like they were watching me. Waiting. Maybe to see what I'd do. And bugger me, even I didn't know what I was gunna do. What would happen when they come in range, was I really gunna shoot at these pricks? What was the use in that? I didn't fancy killing people I never even met. I thought, that's not me, that's bat-shit. And what if there's more nearby? One bit of me said fuck off Jaxie, get clear. But I also had this crazy feeling I needed to see who they were. Maybe they weren't even after me. Then again, meeting anyone at all out here was trouble. I was only safe if nobody knew where I was. Smartest thing woulda been to pull back west into the valley, lose them in the trees. Instead, of course, I moved north. Like someone who couldn't help himself. I had to get one decent look before I legged it.

I went low and quick as I could, zigging and zagging through the trees like I was in me own frigging movie. I couldn't even see the lake properly most of that time. And pretty soon I wasn't even sure where they were anymore. But in the end I come to a little rocky spur above the lake and wormed me way in where I could get the glasses on them.

And then I saw what a fucking muppet I really was.

That wasn't people on the lake. Wasn't even animals. It was a bunch of bloody rocks. All stood up in the salt in curly lines. And it wasn't just a few of them neither, there was heaps of the things. When it finally sunk in I couldn't tell if I was relieved or pissed off. I layed on me front and rested there huffing and puffing, muttering to meself like a mad cunt until me heart slowed down and the head cleared a bit. That's when I got curious again because I still couldn't figure what was going on out there. It wasn't something natural. Somebody'd gone and put that stuff there. Which kinda done my nut in.

They were a lot further away than they seemed. For a while they looked like a fence. Until you got up close and saw they had a kind of tadpole shape with a swirly head and a long tail. Weirdest-looking thing. Hardly one of them rugged slabs was high as your waist.

Before I come out of cover I had one more good look up and down the lake. There was definitely no one out there. Nothing but stones and wavy air. I stood round for a bit to satisfy meself but it was hard to feel satisfied knowing you'd nearly twisted off over a mob of rocks.

Anyway I got going again. Before I did I took a sip and felt how light on the jug was. So it wasn't gunna be the nicest trip back. This was turning into a bit of a mission.

I was halfway to the shore before I saw there was something off about the prints I was following. The treads had changed. And once I paid proper attention I saw the whole shape of the boot was wrong. These ones weren't mine. And fuck me if that didn't come like a kick in the clacker.

I got down on me hands and knees to make sure but it was no mistake. They were some other bastard's bootmarks. And I was like faaark! When I hauled meself up again I looked round slow and careful. Then I backtracked to the stone whatsit and saw another line of prints fanning out at an angle. I walked over and put my steelcap in one and it was me orright. My tracks come as they should from the smudge of trees in the distance. And once I had a proper look it was clear the other trail hived off northish. It wasn't newly made but it was fresh enough to set the hairs up on me. Now even the salmon gums didn't feel safe.

It shat me to have to take another detour. I needed to crack on and make some serious distance. But I couldn't rest easy anywhere if there was someone about. I had to know who they were and how many of them and what the hell they were up to. There just wasn't any choice.

I followed the trail maybe half an hour. It come ashore near some low cliffs made of the same greeny dark stone as out on the lake. Then it headed north again through the saltbush along the edge. Just as I lost it, where the ground got stony, I copped a flash of silver way up ahead. I got the glasses out and saw it, like the shine off a car, a windscreen or something.

That's when I pulled right back off the lake and took to whatever cover the sheoaks and jams give me.

Round then a breeze got up from the east. Or maybe I just noticed it because of the noise in the trees. Whenever I snuck a look I saw them flashes coming quicker all the time. Until I saw it was a windmill. Up beyond that, set in a nest of york gums, was a tin roof with the last sun on it.

The mill might be good news. But a house probably wasn't gunna be. All I could do was hope it was empty. From here I couldn't tell, even with the glasses. I had to think what to do but by then I wasn't feeling so flash. Crampy in the legs. Light in the head.

I scrambled back into cover, got all the kit off of me and drank the last of the water. If there was no trough under that windmill I was in for a shit of a night. I gnawed on some meat but it was caked in salt now and I can't say that helped. I just give meself a spell till the wobbles let up. After that I hauled all me clobber back on and crept in closer. When I smelt smoke I nearly spat it. That's it, I thought, I'm buggered now.

Then I told meself to man the fuck up and stay cool. First thing I had to do was get some water. Everything else, like changing me plans completely, would have to wait. So I pulled back a way to try another angle, get a better view.

I snuck north a bit. Then I come in from the ridge side with my nose into the wind and the sun behind me. Pretty soon I was in close enough to tell it was desert pine burning down there. That's a smell you don't forget.

Further in I come upon a vehicle track. Followed it round a bend where it run past a pit full of rubbish, bent tin, coils of old fencewire, busted chairs, a water tank holey as a flywire door. Half in the ditch was an old LandCruiser stripped to nearly nothing. When I looked over the edge a mob of flies stirred and showed a pile of bones. The ones on top still had streaks of dried meat on them.

I stepped away gentle so I didn't make anything clank and that's when I noticed the wheelmarks. Something was rolling in and out of this camp, and pretty recent too but from what I could see it was on tyres with no treads, which I couldn't figure at all. I got even twitchier after that. Kept following the track in but stayed in the jams and sheoaks alongside, crouching low and stopping every little bit to make sure everything was sweet before I got moving again. And when I saw grey tin through the mulga I got on me belly and crawled in as close as I could, right in under some wattles. Now I was glad of that stinking hot camo jacket. Just had to hope there was no dog. I layed the Browning down careful and took up the glasses, but every time I made some tiny move the pack on me back snagged and swished on branches. So I wriggled out of it slow and quiet as I could. Then I took a proper look at where I was.

It was a corrugated iron hut. Not much bigger than my place

but better built. Had a gable side and a pitched roof with rain gutters, a good tin chimney. In the shade of the verandah were two chairs. Come off a car, from that junked LandCruiser by the looks. Next to them on one side was a door wide open and on the other a window shutter propped out. Along the rest of the front wall was a heap of drums and rusty tools and rope. Plus a wheelbarrow.

It wasn't a new-built place, that's for sure. There was streaks of rust down the roof and the two water tanks were up on stands made of railway sleepers like the olden days. Whoever camped here was no weekend warrior neither because round the tanks I saw old kero tins with vegies growing in them. Back towards me, a bit to the left and clear out in the open, there was a shitcan with the lid shut. And closer still, maybe only ten metres from where I was wormed in, there was a dead tree, a big old gum silver as the hut with a rope slung off it with a pulley and a gambrel that twisted a bit in the wind.

I looked at everything hard and careful as I could. There was no sign of a vehicle, not even a trail bike. So I couldn't figure the wheelmarks at all. It was hard to keep calm. And tough to be this close to water when I was so dry. Man, by then me lips were like tree bark.

This was a pretty organized setup. The hut was in a clear patch of orange stony dirt. Behind the hut, a little way towards the lake, was the windmill. There was a trough at the foot of the tower and round that a fence, a kind of corral made of wire and bushwood. And shit, someone was moving round in there. But when I got a good focus I saw it wasn't a person at all. It was a dirty white nannygoat. And that thing was pissy. It was jumping at the wire, bouncing off the gate, turning circles.

Then I heard a voice inside the hut.

A man.

And the fucker wasn't just talking. He was singing. That day it was like the whole world was out to do my nut in.

I pointed the glasses at the doorway and then the window but it was just black shadow. All I had to fix on was this bloke's singing. And the way he went at it, lunging it out shameless, it was like he fancied the sound of his own voice. Like he's fully fig jam. And fuck me if he isn't singing a song I know. As if me head isn't scrambled enough already. Rare enough you hear a bloke sing but singing a song you actually know, what's the odds? So I'm stuck for a sec, kind of blank, and that's when he steps out barefoot through the open door. I drop the binocs and stare.

It's just an old fella. Mostly bald. Walking dainty like his feet's tender. And still singing. With some things in his hand. He puts them down on a drum. Sits on a milk crate in the shade. Pulls on a pair of gumboots. Then he snatches up the things from beside him and shuffles out in the sun and leans against the verandah post and I see him clear enough. Singlet. Baggy-arse shorts. Thick specs. He's short and thick, this fella. Red in the face. And that stuff in his hand, it's a knife and steel.

He looks round kind of slow and lazy. Stops singing then and just hums a minute while he hones the knife. And he knows how to freshen up a blade, that I can see straight up. When he's done he hangs the steel off a nail in the verandah post and takes up a slip of rope and heaves off down towards the mill. The old black gumboots slop against his shins. That's a sound I know too well. And it's pretty obvious then it's his prints I come across on the salt. But I'm thinking it can't just be him I gotta deal with out here. Can't just be one old man. Because there's no car.

Once his back's turned fully I get the glasses on him and see his big red ears and his hairy shoulders all blotchy with freckles and moles.

I check the goat butting at the fence down under the mill stand. I can see now what the game is. That yard, it's a water trap. Bloke's got it all figured out. Animal smells water in the trough, pushes through the sprung gate and the thing snaps shut behind it. Beats the shit out of chasing roos all over the wildywoods. Way he's gimping along though, cracking the gate like he's sorry to interrupt, this old dude's gunna have his work cut out chasing that grubby white goat round the pen.

But he's quick as a snake. He's hardly through the gate and he's got her. The nanny can't quite believe it. He's snagged her with the noose and it's all over before she can even yank on it. When the knife goes through her throat she sounds like she's laughing. Or maybe that's the bloke. I hope to fuck it isn't me, because I'm cold all of a sudden. Like it's kind of took me breath away.

Really, no shit, I'm frozen stuck. When I shoulda been bolting for the water tank while he's busy I'm laying here watching this goat die on its feet. Giving a shiver and a gurgle and suddenly floppy as a bathmat.

And look, I seen plenty of things killed in me day. Seen cows bolted and pigs necked. Done it meself a heap of times. Stuck them, plugged them with a rifle, took them down with a crossbow. Jesus, I knocked a dog's brains out with a hammer. And I done worse than that too. But seeing this goat go, it give me the horrors. And the mad thing of it is I really did want to laugh. Out aloud. Like some nutbag who can't control himself.

Only time I felt like that before I was still little. It was down in Moora. Nanna was the first dead person I ever saw. She was all layed out on her bed in one of them spotty frocks she liked to wear to the sports club. She had high heel shoes on and stockings. The room smelt of lady powder and Mr Sheen polish and wee. Auntie Marg was in there, sat up next to the bed. She was brushing Nanna's hair with this little baby brush and when I come in, getting kind of pushed in really, with Mum hard up behind me, she reached out the brush and I just looked at it. I didn't know what I was supposed to do. You can brush Nan's hair, she said. I just stared. Nan looked like she was asleep. But she had makeup on and her teeth were in like she was ready to go out.

I was eight then maybe. And I really didn't want to touch her. Hell, I didn't know nothing about brushing ladies' hair. But then the others come in the room, all quiet and a bit sniffly. I couldn't see them but I sure as shit could feel them there, behind me. And I was just stuck looking like a pussy with Auntie Marg holding out this brush and me mum saying me name like she was trying to wake me up. And everyone's watching. So I took the brush. Made a coupla dashes with it near her piggy-pink face. Her hair was blue against the pillow. And when me hand bumped her cheek she was cold and heavy and a kind of spark went through me, like a terrible familiar feeling. And I understood it then. She was meat. That's what dead things are. She was gone but not gone. Meat is something gone and not gone. It didn't feel right. Never really does. And that was it, soon as I felt that porky cold I pushed past them females and went out in the yard that was all dead grass and doublegees and hid behind the laundry shed where no one could see me. Because I was sure I was gunna bawl. I wished that I could of. But all that come out was a laugh that burnt me throat like vomit.

So there I am, laying up under them bushes like a stunned mullet. Not running for the tank, not even creeping back somewhere safer to watch from. Using what energy I got left just to keep me shit together. And then it's too late to do anything at all. Old geezer's hauling the nanny by the legs through the spring gate and out of the little corral. Dragging it one-handed behind him like it never had any more life in it than half a bag of chaff. In his grey singlet and gumboots. With the knife still in his red hand.

He come up by the hut and kept on towards me. I pushed down into the dirt and turned me head aside so he didn't catch my eyes direct. And I should have figured it all along cos he stopped close by. At the silvery dead tree where the rope and gambrel hung.

So I'm caught there while he hoists the goat up and gets on with it. Close enough that I hear him wheeze and fart and talk to himself, though I can't really make out what he's saying and his eyes are hid behind the shine of them specs, but from the start I could see he'd done all this a thousand times before. He starts to hum again. And he's not too shabby with a knife, I'll tell you that for free, because it doesn't take him long to get that nanny skun.

I watched him open the belly and drop its bag right there on the dirt. He got the windpipe and gullet out real quick and pinched off the arse so nothing shat up the meat. Flies on his head like a twinkly crown. He wasn't humming after that. His lips looked pooched up for whistling but I couldn't hear a thing. Then he got a little smile going, like he was pleased with himself or something.

He wiped the carcase down with a rag. Then he shuffled back to the hut and I figured it might be me chance to fuck off, but I needed water so bad I just couldn't. Wondered how long it'd be before a car come down them ruts behind me.

Under the verandah he tipped bushwood out the barrow and chucked in some tools. The barrow was one of them steel-wheel jobbies, like something out of a museum, and there was a long-handled shovel jumping round in it when he rolled it up to the tree.

He worked like there was no rush. Took a cleaver and split the chest nice and clean. Then he set each half on a stump in turn and chomped it into quarters and cuts and he put them all in a hessian bag and strung the lot from the gambrel out of the way of ants. Once he done that he grabbed up all the offal in the skin and slopped it into the barrow with the head and hoofs.

Then, for a second, it was like he was wheeling the thing straight at me. I was pressed to the dirt like a fucking cowpat. Pushed me face into the stones till me bung eye nearly jumped backwards through me head, and even when I heard him veer away and go jangling off in the distance I wasn't game to look up. I waited and counted and counted and waited and it was only when I heard the shovel clang I peeled me face from the ground and saw the cleaver laying on its side on the old gum stump. Down at the verandah that honing steel hung off the post. And his knife was somewhere too. I wanted them things, needed them to stay alive, but I needed water more.

I didn't know if I had time to fill a five-litre jug. Maybe the best I could hope for was a quick dash to the tanks and a suck on one of them taps for as long as I dared. Up to now I'd been so bloody careful. But I was crazy dry.

I got meself ready. Grabbed the Igloo. Figured it didn't weigh nothing to run with if it was empty and if I had more time than I thought I might get it full.

And either he was quick or I was slow because before I was even up off the dirt I heard the barrow rumbling back. So bugger me, that was that. I was wild at meself. Ground me face back into the stones and listened to that barrow rattling, the shovel jangling, the steel wheel hitting every stick and stone along the way. And thought what now, what the fuck now.

Then it was quiet a moment. Like the old man had stopped. To pick something up maybe. I heard him mumble to himself. And I thought, shit I hope he hasn't clocked me. But then he was rolling in again. Close up. By the killing tree. I didn't dare look up but I heard him take down them sacks of meat from the gambrel. I didn't peep till he was back at the hut and clunking round inside.

I saw the dirt under the dead tree, dark as a diesel stain. Flies bristled on it like prickles, like burrs and doublegees. I'm wondering if there's time to make a run for the water while he's in there and then the old prick steps out and grabs an armload of wood from under the verandah. But then he goes inside again and I hear a rattle like a stove grate jerking open. I tense up again, all ready. Only here he is again. With a rag across his shoulder and a lard bucket. And he stands there a minute and says something, plain as day.

To everything a season, he says.

And I'm thinking what the fuck.

Then he says, A time for blood. And a time for soap. Am I wrong?

Talking like he's on TV, the old bugger. Like he's got an audience. And then I think, is he a bit tapped or is he fucking with me? Has he twigged I'm out here?

Then he's off to the mill yard and the trough. And I'm stuck there. Figuring if I can see him at the trough then any move I make for the water tank he'll see me for sure. And if he knows I'm here already he'll be looking out sharp.

If he hadna said anything I woulda tried for sure. That's what I told meself anyway. But really I was snookered. Just laying there like scenery, watching, twitching, trying to get a read on him and racking me brains the whole while, the time it takes him to get there and fill the bucket and slop himself off and scrub his arms and face and wipe with that grey rag and then dip a fresh bucket of bore water and haul it back up, doing everything slow like an old man will do it.

When he's back he leaves the bucket by the door and hangs the rag on a wire strung from the verandah. Then he goes inside and I get ready again to bolt but in a moment he's back with something in his hand. A book. And he sits in the shade on one of them car seats.

And that's it. For the longest bloody time, that's all. After a while the smell of roasting meat gets going but nothing else happens. He just sits there. Reading his bastard book with that poochy, puckered look on his face. Like it's a hell funny book or he's just happy he's got a hunk of goat in the oven. Or maybe he thinks this whole setup is hilarious, me out in the dirt itchy and ant-bit, thirsty as a motherfucker, and him all set with two tanks of water and a feed on the way. No, I tell meself. He won't know, he can't. And I reckon I only tell meself that so I don't jack a round in and blow a hole in him.

So I don't know what to think. But I can see soon enough I'm stuffed. At least till dark I am. There's no way now I'll make it back to the diggings without a drink. So I gotta sit tight till I can sneak one. All night if I have to.

And that's what I did. I never really thought I would have to but that's how it went.

The sun got low. All the shadows stretched out past me towards the hut and crept up to that old man's feet. They were like dogs on their bellies to him. And all he was doing was scratching his balls and reading that book. Now and then it was like he was saying something out aloud from it or just talking to himself. He had this funny way of saying stuff. Like an accent. But also like he was used to talking out aloud. Weirded me out, that. But I stayed put. I knew I could tough him out.

People say I got no self-control, no discipline. Well they don't know shit. I'd like to see any one of them get through a night like that one.

See, a dog knows how to wait. Dogs are good at that. Only because half the time a mutt doesn't even know it's waiting.

Real waiting's when you know you're waiting. But you gotta make yourself like a cattle dog and forget what it is you're doing. I don't mean go to sleep like a kelpie. What I'm saying is you're there but not there. You go somewhere in your head. Otherwise you're fucked. I'm used to that. The way I'm used to being alone.

I know I was sposed to feel sorry for me cousins. But really I was jealous. Because there was three of them. They had each other.

I used to wonder why it was just me on me own but I figured that out. Mum never woulda said it but I reckon by the time she had me she knew what she'd got herself into. Knew what she married, I mean. Maybe the Captain started out decent but he spoiled. Anything with blood in it can probably go bad. Like meat. And it's the blood that makes me worry. It carries things you don't even know you got. Sometimes I wonder if that nasty mean shit is in me too, like he's passed it on. Does that mean I'm gunna be that way? To Lee? And our own kids? Jesus, thinking like that puts the wind up me. To live you gotta be hard, I know that. But nobody wants to be a deadset cunt. That's just not fucking decent.

You might think I'm one heartless prick not caring he's dead but you didn't know him. All I can say is I hope he heard something. Right at the end. The way I used to hear his knife bucket rattle half a second before he come up behind to king hit me.

He was rat-arsed on rum but maybe that night he heard the chassis creak on the Hilux, or maybe the jack made a tiny groan before it give way. So he had one last fuck me moment before it all come down on his head. But that's just daydreaming. Because when you think about it, Wankbag hit the jackpot. All his filthy vicious sins went unpunished. He died quick and easy. Warning or no warning, he went out fast and clean. He was always a mug punter, a waster and a loser all his life, but in the end he got lucky. Luckier than Mum, that's for sure. And that shits me no end.

When I think of Mum now I try to remember her before she got sick. I see her out at the clothesline. Just before a summer storm one time when the Cap was away shooting horses and sawing them up into prime Angus beef. The sky was black and the paddocks the colour of bread. And the wind was up before the rain come in and Mum still had her real hair that was flying behind her. I come out on the back step and she was pulling in the shirts and whatnot and the sheets were rippling and I run over there in me bare feet to help. But I forgot about all the prickles and bindies and doublegees so pretty soon I was hopping round like a dancing poof and we're both of us laughing.

And I'm happy. When she reaches out for me to keep me from falling over I feel like it's my birthday and not even the bruises up her arms can ruin it.

But now she pushes me off and there's a clap of thunder and I think what the hell and she points at the last sheet where there's someone stood behind it. And I think, fuck he's back.

But it's not the Cap at all. I know the shape of that body. With the wind pressing the sheet so close I know who it is. Then the rain pelts down and I'm not even there anymore. All of a sudden I'm in Magnet. And I think, hang on, this didn't happen. I'm in the backyard of the pub and there's a roo hanging from the spinning clothesline, leaking blood onto the grass and jo-jo prickles. I just walk straight past it and up the steps to the big balcony on the second floor. It feels like me feet are full of broken glass but I don't stop until I'm outside their window looking in. Four skinny beds and a fan turning on the scratched up dressing table. None of the others are there, only Lee. Reading a book. In her shorty pyjamas. Her arms and legs all brown from the sun. And the curtain moves every time the fan turns my way so I'm thinking she'll see me any second, I won't say anything, I'll wait for her to see me. Me feet hurt but I don't mind, I could stand there all day. Because she knows I'm there. She's pretending. And it's cool.

But then there's another clap of thunder and she looks up and what she sees terrifies her. For a sec I think it's me she's scared of and it's like a kick in the nuts. But she's looking past me. I hear the rattle. The knife pouch. The steels and blades. The sound of death. I'm half turned round to face him but it's not the Cap at all. It's Auntie Marg. With a knife as big as a fucking sword. And when I put me arm up to stop her the blade takes me whole hand off at the wrist. I think, this woman's gone mental. Then whack, off comes the other hand. You filthy grub, she says. So I belt off down the stairs on me prickle feet and for a moment it's like I'm free and away until

I see what's strung from the clothesline and bleeding out all over the prickles is not a roo at all. It's me. I'm there already, ahead of meself, the little stumps of me arms still twitching against me chest like roo paws. And I think, fuck this, this isn't right.

And then I jerked up a bit and knew I'd dropped off a sec. Next thing I hear the swish of a knife steel and I look out and see the sun's gone. Now the old dude's just a silhouette in front of the hut. Out beyond him the lake's got this weird greeny glow on it. And the smell of roast meat is everywhere and Christ, I can hardly move me legs, it's like they've gone to sleep. I'm wild on meself for drifting off and to make it worse the old geezer starts singing again.

He was his father's only son, his mother's pride and joy . . .

He's standing there, best I can make out, honing his knife, leaning on the verandah post, flashing an edge back before he gets a feed in. And I can't help going dark on him for being so fucking happy with himself.

Then he's gone for a bit, still singing, and a light comes on inside, a lamp or a candle. I hear the oven door. And fuck me, that's a sound you never forget. A bit of clanking round and out he comes again. This time with a hurricane lamp he hangs off a nail. Even without the glasses I can see the tin plate of food, meat and something else. I even see the steam rising off it. The old bugger sets it down on a big old drum and he's still singing.

He robbed the rich, he helped the poor, he shot James MacEvoy.

And it's like every hair on me's up.

A terror to Australia was the wild colonial boy.

Because that's a song Nan used to sing. Heard Mum sing it
a few times too. And sure, I was a bit wigged by then but I got
the idea in me head that this old plonker knew it was a song
would mess with me. Like he knew I was me father's only son.
He didn't just know I was there, he knew who I was, who my
people were. And I thought, you dirty prick. Trying to flush me
out like a stray, putting meat out and playing with me like this.
And then I thought, Jaxie, you knucklehead, how's he gunna
know who you are? He's got no idea you even exist. He's a
lonely bloke talks to himself and sings a lot. People on their
own get like that. So Jesus, man, just straighten up and settle.

So I got meself together. He stopped singing and cut himself
a hunk of meat. And bugger me if he doesn't come out and say,
There's plenty here for two.

And maybe he heard me gasp, because he kept on talking.

I'm a civilized fella, he said.

All I could do was shove me face in the dirt.

But as you see, he said, I'm not a fool. And I hope you're no
more fool than I. So let's be civilized fellas together. There's
food here and you're welcome to it.

I kept me head down. I could feel him waiting. After a bit
I put me head up slow as I could. And that's when I saw the
shotgun behind him on the tarp.

But if you're what's coming to me, he said, then so be it. I'll
go out with my eyes open and my belly full.

Then he started to eat. The plate clunked and clacked. Moths
were mobbing the lamp and the shadows of them danced over

him and the whole front of the hut. I watched him eat the full plate clean. And for a while I thought I might do something crazy. I thought of all them holes in the ground back at the diggings. I had the Browning right there. He was the one in the light, not me. And I had a scope and space enough to get set. By the time he reached for that shotgun he'd be cactus. Out here no one'd hear a thing. There was nothing stopping me.

He chewed and sucked like he didn't have a care, wasn't even sure I was real, and I should of took that as a good sign but it made me boil, like the fucker didn't take me seriously. I was a hungry thirsty beat-up desperate bastard with a .243 and he didn't know how hard he was pushing me. I was so wired by then me teeth felt electric.

For sure he'd twigged to me and now he was foxing. Was he a sly old fucker or some barking nutbag? Maybe he did this every night, thinking he saw things, people who weren't there. But I really was there and he coulda just pumped a few shells off into the dark to make himself feel better, cut me to bits at this range. But here he was offering to feed me.

Well I wasn't falling for it. He didn't know me. Didn't know what I was made of. And he was old. He couldn't stay awake all night. I'd been outwaiting old pricks all me life.

So I was one fucked up individual, it's true, and dirty on him for gaming me like that but I wasn't the sort of person kills a man in cold blood.

Thing is, this old dude couldna known that. He just rolled the dice, didn't he? He wondered if I was a civilized man, like he said. Then he bet his life on it.

But that didn't mean I could trust him. A bloke that doesn't shoot you on sight, a man who offers you a feed, he could still be the one puts you in to the cops.

In the end the old geezer give up and went inside. Maybe he got bored. Or could be he couldn't stand those moths another minute. He et everything on that plate and then some more. And he hummed and sang and sat quiet. Possible he decided he just imagined me. Whatever it was, he packed it in and went inside.

It was late. Well to me it felt like it was. So I figured he'd be getting himself ready for bed. Thought any minute I'd hear him start snoring. But that lamp stayed on. Yellow light fell out the door and through the window shutter. I couldn't see nothing else but whenever I thought the old fella might be asleep I'd hear a chair scrape or a pannikin rattling.

Things itching round in the dirt under me. And overhead

tiny birds or insects give off peeps and shakes and shuffles. Hour after hour I kept waiting for the damn lamp to go out but that old dude was sturdy. It looked to me like that whole hut was ready to doze off. I kept thinking the verandah was starting to droop like an eyelid but I spose that was me.

Sometime in the night a bird dropped into the thornybush above me. I felt the branches twisting and rocking from the landing and then all I heard was flitching and scratching a minute before it lifted off. It never even knew I was there.

Later I had to piss. And it come like a big insult, being that thirsty and still dying to chuck a wiz. So there was nothing I could do but unzip meself and let it go right there. You'd think the dry dust'd soak it up like a sponge. You don't bank on having your duds totally soaked. That was premium, laying in that all night.

I thought about pulling back, slipping up the ridge and finding somewhere safe to sleep, then dragging meself home to the diggings in the morning. People have done harder things than that. And I might of done it. If it hadna been for the smell of water so close and the sight of that shotgun.

I had to wait this out.

I didn't plan on thinking about Lee. This wasn't the time for it. But maybe there was nowhere else to go.

Christmas didn't start out so bad. Up until lunch everything was fine. Mum was pretty crook by then but that day she scrubbed up and acted like there was nothing wrong. She had a yellow dress on and we'd put up tinsel and streamers. In the lounge room there were bowls of snacks everywhere, chips and Twisties, chocolate and stuff. And the house smelt of meat roasting but it was so hot in there and the A/C was on the blink. Auntie Marg was down from Magnet and me and Lee played cricket out the back with the littlies to get some air and keep them busy. It was boring but kind of nice because the old-ies were inside drinking their beers and shandies and Lee and me could be close and the kids didn't know any different.

Now and then a batter would really get onto one and the ball'd go out through the doublegee paddock towards the train tracks and someone'd have to go tippy-toeing through all that shit to get it.

I remember the silos white in the sun. And the smell of stub-ble. Really it was peace on earth and goodwill to all men I was feeling. Especially when the little ones got sooky and went inside for Fanta and it was just us out there on our own.

I had something for Lee, a present I got her. Nothing fancy like the skate wheels but it was something I knew she'd like. Scored it at the tip where all the car wrecks are piled. It's snaky as fuck down there. Half them cars and trucks got king browns crawling through them after the mice. But it's worth the risk if you like collecting badges. I did it more when I was younger, hadn't done it for yonks, but this time it was special. Because round November I found the perfect badge for Lee. Scored it off some truck from the Stone Age. Just the name. In silver running writing. *Austin*. Got it off clean and buffed it shiny.

Glued it to a block of pine I bevelled up and sanded and varnished. Just a badge, I know, but it's right for her because it's her last name. Lee-Ann June Austin.

And I was headed right for the shed where I had it hid when Auntie Marg called us to come and watch a video with the rest of them. So I figured I'd do it later and we went in like good kids, like smiley Christmas cousins. I never did get to give her that present.

It was like this. We're inside, on the couch. Me next to her and the littlies on the floor in front. And the house is so hot and the skin of her leg is cool against mine and I just want to put a hand there. Maybe hold her hand. Because even with the roast going in the oven I can smell that peeled orange smell of her and it's driving me crazy. But old Wankbag is right there in his big recliner, reeking of rum and scratching his beard. And I don't know if I can stand this bullshit another second. Having to pretend, sit there like a dumb animal all day and feel all this stuff and say nothing, do nothing. I didn't want their stupid family Christmas. I didn't want to be with any of them others, didn't even want me own sick mum just then. All I wanted was right next to me and I couldn't have her. And it got too much to take.

So I bolted. Well really I just got up and headed for the door. Auntie Marg said wait Jaxie love, lunch'll be ready in a minute. But I kept on going and I'm in me bare feet across that prickly grass and past the washing line to the shed and I get inside the shade but the whole place stinks of him and I'm all wild and panicky like I'm trapped and so I push through the little back door and out into the hard sun and the snaky weeds behind.

I'm stuck there. Like I don't know what I'm doing, can't think what to do. I've got no shoes. I can't go running out into them stubbly paddocks. All the firebreaks are bristling with doublegees. And the train tracks are so hot they'd melt the bottom off your feet. I've got a horn you could hang a waterbag off and it's terrible, stupid, humiliating and I don't know if I should have a wank or slice it off with a box cutter. And that's how she finds me, bawling me eyes out hard and silent and horrible. I can smell her right beside me but I can't even look at her. But she isn't bothered. She puts her hands on me gentle, on me face, me ears, and she kisses me and makes this tiny noise like she's trying to stop a baby crying but I can't stop, I'm helpless, I'm so ashamed. And you know all I really wanted right then wasn't to get in her pants, I just wanted to say all this stuff I couldn't get out. It was like I could say her name with me mouth but not with me voicebox. I thought I was gunna burst into flames and die.

And next thing she's kneeling in the dry weeds. For a second I think she's begging me to stop crying, stop all this fish-face gulping shit. But she pulls me shorts down. Her hair's shining. Them strange eyes are looking up into me like she understands everything. And it wasn't like any time before because it was so sad and calm and kind and it was like we really were in a room of our own. When I was done she squatted back on her haunches and wiped her mouth with a victory grin and that's when I knew I would love her forever, that I'd do anything to keep her and save her and nothing they could do to me would make me give up on her.

Next thing of course he's standing there, winding one up. And I can see the fist coming but I don't even move to save meself.

I went down in the weeds face first and all I could think was that the whole earth smelled of Lee and that was right and good. And when I got up they were both gone.

I come into the kitchen and it's dead quiet. Everyone's up round the table with silly paper hats on and they're waiting, hardly breathing by the looks. The grub's all out, the meat and vegies, the gravy and drinks. There's streamers and tinsel everywhere. But no one's happy. It's like they've all forgot what they're doing there. Me little cousins have this scared puzzly look on their faces. Mum and Auntie Marg have got their hands over their mouths, eyes as big as oven dials. And of course he's the one not sitting. He's back against the sink in his new Hawaiian shirt necking a bottle of homebrew, and he pulls the bottle off his mouth and burps and just looks at me.

You filthy grub, he says.

I say nothing. Me head's still ringing. Then Lee comes in, face hot and wet. Like she's been in the bathroom. Trying to figure out what to do. Auntie Marg makes a noise like she's gunna yack.

When he comes at me I turn to run. Then I'm crawling in glass and beer. And he's talking. He says it all. Even in front of the little ones. What we did. What he saw. Even though he must of said something like it already. And the women are screaming. Not for what he's doing to me. No, fuck me, never for that.

Then Auntie Marg's across the room and she's got Lee by the hair. The kids are running out the door. Lee looks at me one time. She has them cut-off shorts on and a T-shirt showing the sweat in patches all up her front. Her feet are bare. But it's them slaughterhouse eyes I remember.

And that was the last time I was in the same room as her. She wasn't even allowed to come to the funeral.

But this isn't how I want to think of Lee. When I bring her up out of the dark I put her in a big fat chair in a room with curtains. She's wrapped in a sheet with her hair grown back and combed back wet like she's just got out of a bath. This isn't some cheapshit room in the Railway. This is five star. Deep carpet. There's food and flowers everywhere, cold chicken and pizza, bottles of champagne or something, all on trays and tables. She sits back like a princess with her dirty bare feet up on the end of a bed that's wider than a swimming pool. And she's doing her eyebrow thing at me the way she does, to get me to laugh when I'm trying to look serious. I'm all clean and dressed right, like a grownup man. Me pockets are full of money. But I can't keep it together. I fall down laughing. On me face, down onto the bed, into all that food. With her.

II

I woke up with something at me, poking, digging. Like an animal. And I jerked up so quick I snagged me head in all them snarly branches.

Well, the old bloke said, peering in, holding onto his spastic-looking rodeo hat with its curly sides. Good morning to you, then.

He straightened. Twisted a stick in his hand a sec and threw it aside.

I didn't say nothing, I just blinked. It took me a bit to catch on. And when I reached for the rifle he smiled and lifted his shoulder so I could see the Browning strapped across it already. He pushed that cowboy hat back off his face.

Quite a night, wouldn't you say?

When I opened me mouth it made a dry tearing sound. Like the noise a hide makes coming off a beef.

A rough one for the both of us, he said.

I didn't have the spit for words. Didn't know what to say anyhow.

I thought you were the end of days. I admit it, for a while I really did. But then I asked myself, would they send a child? Of course they would!

Then he laughed in a way that wasn't real funny. And I couldn't figure out what the fuck he was talking about. I just looked at him through the thornybush and saw the sky all eggy behind him and it come down on me hard what I done. I went the whole distance, waited all night. Jesus, I made a fucking warrior of meself to hold out and I've gone and nodded off at the end. And now I've let meself get caught.

An urchin, no less, he said.

He reached in and got hold of me waterjug and I couldn't help edging back a bit. I was burred up and narky as a feral cat. I figured whatever was coming next it wouldn't be good. And I didn't have anything left to go him with.

Then he shook the jug and laughed.

For what does he thirst, this youth in the wilderness? Streams of living water? Or perhaps it's vengeance.

I couldn't tell if he was off his tits or taking the piss. I didn't say nothing. I thought to meself, I'll never see Lee again. If he doesn't bury me out here he'll dob me in to the cops.

Will you not give a fella good morning? Nothing to say for yourself? After a drink, perhaps. Come on with ye.

I figured what the hell. I wasn't too steady on me feet but once I was up and into the clearing I went straight for the tank and got on me knees. I didn't care he was behind me with the gun. All I could think about was water. It was warm as blood and I swallowed hard and fast as I could and when I couldn't keep up I let it run over my face and down me neck until the old bloke reached across and cranked the tap shut. For a while I just layed there in the sticky dirt and I could feel him standing back to watch.

Worse than I thought, he said.

Then he stepped over and give me one arm and like some little kid I took his hand and got up swaying. He didn't let go right away. Instead he turned me hand over and looked up me arm and saw all the flakes of dry blood.

That's quite a musk you've worked up, he said.

I didn't know what he was on about so I didn't say nothing.

You'll feel better after a soak.

A drink is all I wanted, I said.

And you're welcome to it, lad. But look at the state of ye. Those duds could walk to the laundry house unassisted.

That's when I copped to what he was saying, that I stunk. I flashed up at that. Angry mostly but I was embarrassed too. And there was nothing I could do or say because it was his water going through me gut like a hot worm while I stood there and I was wobbly as a poddy calf.

There's soap down at the water yard, he said. And a towel I can offer you.

Whatever, I said.

Ah, he said. That's the spirit.

I didn't want a wash. I just wanted a lay down in the shade. And it weirded me out it was such a big deal to him, I didn't like it one bit, but he was the one with the gun so what was I gunna do? I took his towel and went down to the mill with him behind me. The yard round the trough was fixed over with so many twitches of wire it looked like a mad lady's knitting. The gate was rough as guts but when I pulled it back a little I saw the spring was still good. I wondered how many goats this old dude had seen off. And how many dickheads like me. On a stump in there next to the trough was a tin bucket and a squeezy bottle of soap. The old man waved me in like it was a table full of food he had ready.

Give those duds a good laving, too, while you're there. All of it. They'll dry soon enough, and I have some spares for ye.

I spose I stared at him. He just raised up his eyebrows and grinned, like I should get on with it. But I sure as shit wasn't gunna drop me dacks in front of some stranger.

You go ahead, there. I'll make us some tea.

I waited till he was halfway back to the hut before I even pulled me boots off. I stood at the gate a moment. Wondered if I was any smarter than a wild goat. And then I pushed at the gate and went in.

The ground under me feet was spongy with goat poop. The damp come right up through me socks. I looked at the greeny insides of the trough a minute, hung me cap on the fence, set the phone on top of the post and climbed in with all me clothes on. I didn't know what this old joker was into but if he was bent that way I sure as hell wasn't gunna make it easy for him.

And Christ, was the water cold. It was hard and brassy like the water from the rez and when I yelled I heard him laughing all the way up the track. I thought fuck you, old man. Laugh at me. But same as at the rez, the cold give off a buzz after a while and then me body warmed up to it and for a moment I floated, like the whole of me was free.

When I come up later he had a fire going on the ground out front of the hut and his big black billy was nearly at the boil. The old man looked at me standing barefoot in the towel and he seemed too shocked to be pervy. I spose I was in pretty bad shape then. Apart from the scratches and divits I caught along the way, there was the bumps and bruises I left home with. I hadn't planned to take me gear off at all but with them cold clothes hanging off me I got the mighty shivers, so I shucked them soon as I got out of the trough and I hung them on the windmill. A rub with the rough towel did some good but it was only the fire out in the yard that got me feeling human again.

By God, he said. Looks as if you fought your way here tooth and nail.

I didn't say nothing to that. I had the phone wrapped in me hat and I clamped it hard in front to keep the towel up. I stood in to the fire till it felt like the hairs on me legs would go up in flames. The old man went in the hut. He come out with a tin bowl in one hand and some clothes in the other.

Here, he said.

I took the duds but I wasn't about to put them on there and then.

Of course, he said. Step inside, there.

He put the bowl on the dirt and I saw it was full of flour dough. He sat on a milk crate and pinched off a handful and flattened it out a bit and set it on the ashy coals, to one side. It seized up in the heat and give off a smell too good to believe in. I watched till I couldn't stand it anymore.

Inside the hut it was dim. Same cement floor and stud walls as my prospector's shack but it was roomier and better built and he sure as hell had more stores. He had a tin sink and bucket under the window next to the wood stove. There was no glass in the window, just a shutter pushed out on a pole. An old iron bed and mattress. A table. Two chairs. In pine crates stacked against one wall he had books. And along the jarrah noggins all round there were rocks and shells and bird nests and bits of bone. The best thing of all was the meat safe. Really just a fly-wire cupboard. Painted green once by the looks but the colour was gone all milky. Each of its wooden feet was in a tin of water to keep the ants out. It was perfect. For half a second I saw meself lugging it back up the lake and over the ridge to where I had the roo hanging. But how could that happen? What was I gunna do, steal it from him?

Me rifle was stood against the wall inside the door but the mag was gone and my guess was the chamber was empty. I couldn't see the shotgun anywhere.

In the end I got into them old man shorts and pulled on the

shirt. Both smelled of woodsmoke and something lemony and familiar. Near the door there was a little shaving mirror but I didn't want to look. I put the cap on and stuck the phone in the pocket of the shorts and when I walked it thumped against me leg.

Out at the fire the old bloke knocked the grit and ash off the damper and give me half. He poured tea into two pannikins and give me one. I waited as long as I could but I still burnt me mouth on the tea. I dogged the damper down in three big bites and the old dude laughed and give me the rest of his. He grabbed up another batch and set it on the coals. And for a while we neither of us said nothing. Him sitting, me still standing. It was weird.

Then he said to get meself a chair and I told him I was orright like I was. He clacked his teeth together like I'd pissed him off a bit and after a coupla moments he pointed at me eye and said, That's a mighty shiner there.

I shrugged.

You're a brawler, then?

I sipped me tea.

Not so many doors to be walking into out here.

I just sniffed. I didn't know what he was on about.

So, he said, you're out hunting and you get yourself turned around somehow and you lose the others, and so here you are, no?

If you say so.

Whatsay?

I said if you say so.

Hmm, he said. Do you not say so yourself, then?

Why d'you want to know? I asked him.

Well, now, I'm a curious fella, he said still smiling.

I didn't say nothing to that and he looked me over again like he was trying to decide something. Behind his specs his eyes swum like two fat fish. Restless fish.

Put yourself in my shoes, lad, I'm out here alone and I see no man from one month to the next and when some fella comes creeping up on my place unannounced I get a burning interest in what his provenance is, what the caper is, what his fecking story might be. You understand me?

All I did was shrug and chew on me damper and look into the coals of the fire.

It was your glasses gave you away, anyroad, he said. The binoculars, or the rifle sight. Just so you know. I caught a flash down there to the south. A gentleman on his own notices things, and out here an event is a premium phenomenon. So I kept me auld eyes peeled, as they say in the fillums, and there you were again, in closer but up towards the ridge. You were out by those stones on the salt yesterday, am I right?

I nodded.

Something to behold, wouldn't you say?

You knew I was here the whole time?

Oh, I had a notion. A man alone reverts to his animal nature, lad. Don't you agree?

I dunno. Maybe.

That's not to say he becomes a beast, now.

I thought of that scattergun again. I knew I could be dead

already, or bleeding and full of pellets.

So, like a creature of the wild, I felt you out there, he said. Sensed your presence, felt you watching. Good God, boy, it's a wonder I didn't smell you as well, given the state of you. And there's the small matter of your knapsack – I can see it from here even now.

I looked up past the killer tree and the gambrel to the thorny-bushes where I was hid all night and there it was, plain as all fuck, a flash of blue against the green and grey.

Jesus, I said, disgusted with meself.

But I'm still a civilized man, you know, and a man needs more than scents and shadows to make sense of the world. A fella needs a story. Don't you think?

I watched him turn the damper with a twitch of fencewire. The smell of burnt flour give me the headspins.

Go on, now, he said. That was your cue.

What? I said.

Tell a poor auld fella your story, why don'tcha.

Nothing to tell, I said.

Whatsay?

I said nothing to tell.

You're not lost, then?

Not really.

Eh? he said turning his head at me like he wasn't hearing right.

I'm not lost, I said.

So who sent you?

Nobody.

Then how in hell's teeth did you get here?

Walked, I said.

Pshaw!

I shrugged.

Walked from where, the highway?

Further, I said.

How much farther?

Doesn't matter, I said, knowing I'd spilled too much already. I didn't want to be leaving any trail of breadcrumbs back to Monkton. I didn't know who he might know there.

You stole a car, then? How old are you, boy?

I didn't steal any car, I told him.

It's of no account to me, lad, I'm not the law. I see the state of you.

I come on foot. All the way.

All the way from where?

I looked away from him and into the ash and coals and the ants coming round to snaffle the crumbs.

And you just happened to find me. In all this forsaken wilderness.

Didn't even know anyone was down here, I said.

So what's your game? he said, getting all hot. Why might you be here? What's your purpose?

That's my business, I told him and I got sharp as I could then, ready to fight if he come at me. I figured he was old and I was young and he was still sitting and I was on me feet. I knew if he come for me I had to get him first.

But now it's my business, too, you see.

Bullshit, I said.

The point is you came from somewhere.

That shit don't matter.

And you're headed somewhere.

Jesus, who cares?

Oh, I'd say we both do.

The old tool got all smiley again and hooked up his damper and set it on a coupla sticks to cool. Then he rubbed his silvery whiskers. I really couldn't make him out. And I didn't know if I should stand down or stay fierce. The only thing he had for a weapon was that bit of fencewire but then he set it on the dirt and scratched his head with both hands and sighed.

Well, now, he said in the end. If that's your story, I'd say you either lack imagination or you're short on generosity. You're all middle, it would seem. No beginning, no end. You disappoint me.

I needed salt, I said without meaning to.

Oh? Salt is it now?

I wanted salt to keep me meat. That's all. I seen your roof and come up to check it out.

To check me out.

Look, I got no beef with you. I had a gun too you know. I coulda done things if I was like that.

And you're not like that?

No.

You had the means to do me harm, I grant you that, and you refrained. Which is why I wondered if you'd come bearing a message.

No message, I said.

Ah, he said, softening up like he was baffled all of a sudden and a bit bummed. No message.

Didn't mean to give you a fright.

Well, you're a mystery, then, he said, picking up the damper again and pulling it in half and passing me one bit. But I've had my fill of mysteries.

I et the piece slowly to show him I wasn't some kind of savage. Maybe to show meself too. He looked at the damper in his hands and turned it over like it was something might have clues in it.

Sometimes it's a mighty struggle to know what's real and what's just . . . a mirage. You understand?

Yeah, I said.

In a place like this, alone, oftentimes you wonder. And it's hard to know what to trust in. So *you* are quite a conundrum.

A what?

You're something of a problem, lad.

I don't have to be, I said. I'm not gunna say anything. About you, this, whatever it is you're doing.

How will I know that?

Because I said I won't. Why would I? I don't want the grief. Hell, I dunno who you are, what you're up to, really I don't give a fuck. I got me own shit to get done. I never seen you and you never seen me, end of story.

You really don't know my name?

No bloody idea, I said with me mouth full.

Is that the truth?

I nodded.

And does the truth mean something to you? That is to say, is it important? Have you been lied to, have you had lies told about you?

I stopped chewing then. I had a cold feeling come over me. Like he could see into me.

I'm telling the truth, I said

Well, I'll have to take you at your word, lad.

And I'll have to take you at yours.

Yes, he said, distracted.

When you give it to me.

Whatsay?

I said when you give me your word. You dunno who I am, you never saw me.

Of course.

Orright then.

And then he looked into the fire a while.

So, you really didn't come here for me?

Fuck, man, I just told you.

Not even a confounded message?

No, I said. There was no one sent me.

He bit on his damper and et it like an old geezer will, like his teeth and gums were sore, like he was trying to chew sand and ball bearings. And there was something went out of his eyes. I couldn't tell if he was relieved to hear nobody sent me or if it was the worst news of his life.

Am I sposed to know who you are? I asked him. Like, are you famous or something?

No, he said. I'm nobody. Please God, whatever I was I am no longer. And it could be that none of it rates now. All is forgotten, if not forgiven – it could have come to that. But I don't trust the thought. I don't know if it's because it would be too easy or too terrible to imagine no one cares anymore.

I didn't follow him. So I didn't say nothing. The damper was good and the tea was even better. And he was right, the bath done me good but it all made me sleepy as a baby. I looked away to the crap he had stashed under the verandah, the coils of rope, the axe and sledge, the swag under the sheet of corry iron.

You see, he said peering into the smoky coals, they send children out to do what a man wouldn't do. Fill them with drugs and arm them to the teeth. And it's not just Africa, not just these days, either – they've been doing it since Cain and Abel. I truly thought you were the end of days.

I guess he copped me looking at him like he was a fucking nutburger because he give a little laugh and stopped.

My name is Fintan, he said. Fintan MacGillis.

Have you been to Africa then? I asked.

Who's asking, now?

Forget it, I said.

Not if you'd been there, you wouldn't.

I stared at him a while. I couldn't figure him out in a fit.

Our stories. We store them where moth and rust destroy.

I tipped me dregs on the dirt and kept me mouth shut.

We're precious about them, no? Not because we treasure them at all, but because it's safer to hold them close. Am I reading you right? Do we have that much in common?

I turned the pannikin in me hands and looked away from him.

There you are in your beginning, and here am I near my end.

Me name's Jackson, I said. Jaxie Clackton.

There it is.

Yeah, I thought. You fucking idiot, you've done it now. And could be he was thinking exactly the same thing. We'd shown ourselves, said our names. We'd both of us near as hell given ourselves away.

I never did know what to make of Fintan MacGillis. In the end you could say I knew what kind of man he was and maybe that was the important thing. He was Irish, he told me that straight up. But I never found out what it was he done to get himself put there by the lake, what kind of person he was before. Not really. He let things slip, but he never give me the whole beginning and middle. Like he said, I showed up at the end and that was plenty enough for both of us. It's only now I get what he meant. He was one of them geezers been out on his own so long he talks to himself all day, tells himself what he's about to do, what he should do, what he's forgotten to get done. He talked so fucking much it was like a junkpile he chucked at you. You had to sort through all these bent up words to figure which was bullshit and which was true. What I mean is he made a lot of noise but sometimes he didn't say much. With that accent of his and the way he said things fancy and musical, it was like camouflage and you knew deep down he'd been doing this all his life, hiding in clear sight.

He had a boozer's face but as far as I could see there was nothing to drink out here but rainwater and billy tea. He had skinny legs with ropey blue veins winding up them and his top teeth were plastic and they moved enough to make you seasick. His specs was always on crooked too, one hinge busted and the arm wired on rough as a pig's tit. And it was clear he was half deaf. Anytime you said something he cocked his head like a kelpie.

That first day we sat out there all morning, it felt like. When the damper was gone he tickled up the fire again and went back to poking and prodding questions at me like he could stoke me just as easy. But I was careful. I didn't want him knowing anything in case others come through and put the hard word on him. I figured I'd be back down at the diggings for a few weeks.

He said his place was an old shepherd's hut from the days when they ran sheep on this country. I asked him who owned the land and he said he didn't know, but I reckoned he knew once and things had changed. People are always talking about the damn Chinese buying up land but it could have been anybody. Whoever owned it now, they were in no hurry to do anything with it. There was no stock, no machines, no people. Just him and me and a few wild goats.

I asked him did he have a phone or VHF and he laughed at

me. Said he saw I had a phone. I said there was no signal. So we was square there. Then I asked him about his car and he told me there was no car, he'd never had a car out here. And that was when I copped on a bit. Like he really wasn't any hermit prospector or weekend warrior popping goats for fun. And he sure as hell wasn't on any kind of holiday up here in the salt country. He was like some sailor put off on an island in the middle of nowhere. This fella was marooned.

That was weird. And interesting. I was pretty curious about him. But really I was more keen to pull me gear together and get going. If he'd let me. Because it was still him calling the shots, far as I could see. So I watched and waited. And he just sat on by the fire like he was thinking. It was kind of out there. Me squirming about in his flappy shorts and shirt, in me bare feet, wondering what the fuck next.

Then he stirred and got up and started into making tea again. He hummed and grunted and talked under his breath. And then he let off a fart.

Oh, he said. Manners.

Don't look at me, I told him.

Whatsay?

Nothing.

I do beg your pardon, he said. I forget myself.

So how long you been here? I asked him.

Oh, he said hoiking tea leaves on the dirt. A long time. Years.

Like how many years?

Oh, eight? Yes, I think eight.

And you walked here too? I asked, even though I could see

he couldn't possibly of walked here with all this shit he had.

No, he said. Of course not. I was delivered. Which is a slippery word, is it not?

You mean someone brung you out here?

They did.

With all this stuff?

He nodded.

From where?

As you surely know, son, it doesn't really matter.

They just left you out here?

Aye.

Jesus.

Indeed. But this is refuge as much as exile. You might say I find myself a captive at large. Have you read your man Dostoevski, then? Do they teach him at school?

I shook me head.

A pity.

Too much stuff.

And he tipped his head which was scaly and ginger-looking like he'd copped more sun than a fella like him was designed for.

Whatsay?

I said you got too much stuff. You didn't come here with food for eight years.

No, no. Someone comes. Easter and Christmas. In the main. In the main.

Who? Who does?

Whoever they are, Jaxie. You hardly need to know. I thought

we understood each other.

Well orright. But shit.

Twice a year someone comes with food and necessities, a few books, a little news. But Easter has been and gone and, well, nobody. So.

What happens if they don't come at Christmas?

Well, we'll see then, won't we?

I didn't feel it was a good moment to tell him I wouldn't see at all. Because I wasn't gunna be here at Christmas. Man, that was months and months away.

By now, he said filling up the pannikins, a man should have learnt that nothing is certain. This is what I tell myself, of course, but it's an effort to discipline the mind. A fella can't help pining for a bit of solid ground. So I take quare comfort when the sun pops up there across the lake every morning and the roof is on and there's a goat in the yard. I tell myself, here it is, another today – surely this is enough. But the feeling, sad to say, it doesn't last. You see, even a man with no future gets himself into conniptions of . . . of anticipation. What next? When will it be? Will they come? Is that all? What will happen?

And then he went off into one of them long quiets. He chewed his plastic teeth and I listened to the spinifex pigeons coming and going and blew on me tea and drank it quick as I could. After a while of this I figured it was worth trying to bust a move.

Listen, I said, getting up and chucking me dregs, I got some ground to cover.

What? he said. Now?

He looked me up and down like he only just remembered I was there.

I have to get back, I said.

Back where?

Me camp.

Ah. Yes. And where is this bivouac?

South, I said. I left a roo hanging. It'll be nearly on the turn.

Oh, a slab of kangaroo, now what I wouldn't give for that. The goats have been the saving of me, Jaxie, but oh the monotony.

I could bring you some now and then, I said, not really sure if I meant it. Swap you maybe.

He waved me down again but I stood there, restless and nervy.

Your laundry, he said. It won't be dry.

No odds to me, I said, even though I hate hiking in damp duds, and wet socks suck to the shithouse.

Stay for lunch, he said. There's meat left, more than enough.

Nah, I said. I'll get going.

You hardly look well enough.

I'm fine, I said, but I was feeling pretty rooted and everything was sore.

Well, he said, before you go, would you do an auld man a favour, Jaxie?

Depends, I said.

I need to be getting in some wood, you see. Whatsay we get in a barrowload? Then I'll pack you some goat.

Well, I said with a shrug. Orright. I'll go get me boots.

No need, he said. I have some here for you. Give your things a little longer to dry, anyroad.

It felt weird enough already being in his clothes. Still, I sat on a crate under his verandah, with no socks, pulling on a strange pair of boots. He had the .243 on his shoulder and I didn't want to rock the boat.

So we pushed the barrow up the track a way, well I pushed it and he yammered on next to me, and his boots felt heavy and crooked and the ruts looked wavy and a coupla times I thought I wasn't quite right, but it wasn't bad enough I'd puke. It was gunna be a nice old trip back to the diggings feeling this ordinary.

We got out past the junkpile and into a mob of salmon gums and jams where the ground was jumbled with sticks and ant-eaten limbs and it didn't take long to fill the barrow. I felt better heading back in and the old man was poxing on about how we were near enough to being neighbours and if I was to come by one day with a feed of roo it was best we had ourselves some kind of signal, like a call or a whistle. When he asked me did I know a bird noise we might use I couldn't think what to tell him, so I give out the noise of a shithawk and he laughed like a loony and said that was perfect. Said whenever I come by I should hang back in the bush and do the birdcall and he'd know it was safe, and I said fair enough just for something to say when really I didn't give a rat's ring.

When we come by the killing tree I set the barrow down and went into the scrub to get me pack and glasses and jacket. And I thought he'd take up the load and wheel it in himself but he come along with me, nattering all the way. When I bent in to pick everything up the ground went soft under me and I fell to me knees. He said something behind me I couldn't properly hear and I thought right then, you old prick, you've drugged me.

You been clobbered enough you know the feeling. The world's a long way off, fizzing outside of you like a bad TV signal. It's like when you get a boot from an electric fence and everything's wavy and dotty for a bit and then after a minute or so the world comes pouring back in. I spose I was like that. I could smell blood and meat and sawdust and I thought, fucking hell, I've been poleaxed again, I'm gunna kill the cunt.

And then there's clanging and some bastard singing and I open me eyes and over me there's corry iron and jarrah beams and woodsmoke all round. The smell of desert pine burning. And the ground's luxury soft under me. So I blink and turn me head real careful and there's orange dirt and a puddle of ash and the killing tree and everything out front of the shepherd's hut. But the shadows are all wrong. Like it's afternoon already.

What the fuck?

I sat up and cracked me arm against the tin wall and Fintan MacGillis stuck his head round the doorframe.

So, how ye?

What'd you give me?

Whatsay?

What the fuck you do to me?

Well, I got you on the barrow, more or less. We'll collect the wood later.

You give me something!

Tea and damper, I believe. And I'm after getting some chops on if you're still hungry.

I was parked on a swag under the verandah. I didn't remember getting there. But I knew I was hungry. Christ, I was hole in the guts starving.

Took a bit of a turn there, lad. Dehydrated is my guess. Are ye well now?

I spose, I said.

Fact was I had a bastard headache but I didn't feel so woozy.

What's Magnet?

What?

Something you were saying, is all.

Nothing, I said. It's nothing.

He pursed his lips like he didn't believe me but wasn't gunna push it.

It's afternoon, I said, getting up. It's late.

I leant against the verandah post and remembered I wasn't

in me own clothes. When I patted the pockets of them shorts there wasn't any phone.

It's in here on the table, said the Irishman.

You fucking took it?

Fell from your pocket, Jaxie. Don't be getting ahead of yourself, now. It's here with all your other kit.

And you had a good stickybeak I bet.

Steady now. You don't want to be losing a friend here, not when you're short of them already.

He give me that fuck-you grin and then I knew the old bastard had been through me phone. He'd had half the fricken day to scroll through me pics and messages. His eyes and fingers had been all over Lee, across me whole bloody life. He'd seen her with her head shaved when it was raw and ugly and that was worse than if he seen her stripped naked. Jesus, I coulda popped his eyeballs out with me own two thumbs right then, I coulda strangled him with a hank of fencewire.

I've opened a tin of mushrooms for the occasion, he said, sweet as cupcakes. And there's still the odd tomato.

I wanted to tell him to shove the lot of it up his freckle and set fire to it but the talk of food made the inside of me mouth twitch.

Your duds're dry, he said.

He went back inside and I heard the stovetop clank and something started hissing in a pan.

I went round to the tank and took a long suck from the tap like I should of the night before and I looked at the greens growing in kero tins and tomato plants crowded up against the wall. The easterly was petering out to nothing when I went down the mill in them slope-sided boots of his, the blades of the thing was hardly turning. The lake was gone pink with the evening sun and a mob of birds stretched across the sky like a scratch. I felt so flat. And stupid. I thought of all that roo meat on the turn back at the diggings. Even if I got going there and then, no way would I be getting back to me own place tonight. I'd be lucky to make it the day after.

I got all me clobber on and pulled on dry socks and proper boots at last. Then I brung his gear back to the hut and the place was full of frying smoke and me mouth just run with spit, so that was that.

We et sitting at the table and for once the old man didn't say nothing. The hut wasn't so gloomy with the sun piling in through the open door and the shutter above the sink. I still had some of that stunned feeling hanging on but the food perked me up. He had those rack chops fried up hard and salted and crusty. I gnawed every one of them down to the speary bit of bone and he watched me like I was something on TV.

When I was finished and he was making a brew I looked round at his boxes and stacks of tins. Fintan MacGillis had powdered milk, sugar, cans of butter, bags of flour in plastic tubs, dried peas, kerosene, cooking oil. He was set up pretty good, even if his mates didn't come again till Christmas. There was a pile of goat meat in the safe. For all I knew he had more salted down in them plastic barrels pushed into the corner.

And I dunno why but I thought after eight years living out here he might have put photos up, but all he had was books and some pictures cut out of magazines. There was one of a little white house with soft green grass all round it and a thatch roof. Another one was a dude black as the night standing in a boat up to his knees in fish and he's laughing his tits off. He had big flat teeth like a hippo and they was stained red like he'd been eating meat raw off the bone. And there was one more picture of a pair of dirty sandals, just sandals on dry cracked mud, that was it. All them cut-outs, he had them glued on bits of packing case or cardboard and hung on nails and they were bubbly and wrinkled like he'd made the paste himself the way we used to when we was kids.

The old man's books were stood up in a fruit crate and in front of that, layed out flat, was this necklace thing or a bracelet maybe, made of coloured beads, blue, red, green, orange, yellow, white, black.

You make that? I said, pointing to it.

No, he said. I did not.

He give me a pannikin of tea and he sat back down and drunk his slow and methodical. I looked back at that bead thing on the shelf. It was way out of place in a hut like this, in an old dude's stuff, and he could see me sussing it out and I thought for sure he'd get on his hind legs and say fifty-nine things about it but the look on his face said that wasn't gunna happen, like it was off limits.

Good chops, I said.

How old are you, son?

Seventeen, I told him.

Closer to fifteen, he said. That's my guess.

You can guess all you like.

A perilous age to be out here alone, wouldn't you say?

I shrugged. I looked at the plate and lined all me chop bones up.

But I see you're a handy lad, he said. It's not every boy who can keep himself alive. At fifteen I still needed me mam to do for me. But she sent me off anyroad. They all did, the mams, and what a quare pack of goms we were, Jaxie. Nobody was giving the likes of us a Browning rifle, either, not out our way. We had to settle for the fear of God, boiled cabbage and the comforts of the strap.

He went quiet for a bit. Then he looked at me as if he'd forgotten I was there.

Have you far to go?

I nodded.

But it'll be dark in an hour.

I'll get far as I can and camp up.

With not even a blanket to your name?

Done it plenty of times, I said.

You'd be safer after a night's rest. You're worn out.

You want me to stay here?

If you fancy. You'll be the better for it. There's space enough.

I thought of another night in the salmon gums. This wasn't exactly what I had in mind when I come down for salt. A fuck-up was how it felt. And this failed feeling come down on me and I knew I didn't have it in me to set off now.

Okay, I said. Maybe I will. Just for tonight.

Well, he said. You're very welcome.

And then I got up and stood in the door. Because the food was done and I'd said I'd stay and now I didn't know what to do. I felt so rotten I could cry. But I didn't cry.

Lad, are you well?

Fine, I said with me back to him.

Do you feel strong enough to walk a little way?

Where?

This time of day I like to take a step on the lake. Not far. For the kindly light, you know. And to see what the lake might do.

It's a salt lake, I said. It can't do nothing.

Ah, but it moves all day, he said. It's forever changing.

I turned back to him. He had this idiot look on his face.

Have you not seen it crawl upon itself and fill and empty in the afternoons? Now and then, you know, I see the eastern shore in the sky, all those stunted trees standing on their heads above the desert.

That's mirages, I said.

Mebbe so, he said. But there's life in them.

And he got up and pushed past me into the light which was gone all milky.

Come on, Jaxie, lad, I'll show you.

I don't know why I followed him. Coulda been because I was feeling so low and shitty. Or maybe just to shut him up. But also because he left the rifle behind. He waited outside a sec and it was just two of us equal. And I thought, fuck it, fair's fair, he's being decent.

And that's how we went, two people side by side. And it wasn't far we went. Past the windmill, out through the samphire and onto the lake a little way.

The old man was in no hurry and that suited me fine. He slopped along in his gumboots and the going was easy. Except he kept bloody talking. It was like he couldn't stop himself. I went along next to him feeling a bit sorry for meself again and wishing he'd shut up. We stopped walking soon enough but the talk, that never dried up

Will ye look at this, boy. What a picture! What a provocation!

I pulled up right beside him and looked out at the salt and the sky and the wafty light between.

I used to think it was Hell itself. This place I'd been consigned to. The heat and salt and flies. A place so empty a fella's thoughts come back from it as echoes. Look out there, now, how it goes on forever, like a dream there's no escaping. Can you imagine how it might have seemed to the likes of me? Terrible, strange, inhuman. And those mirages, by God, they haunted me. Every one a distortion, a travesty. Some days I used to think the lake, the salt, the whole countryside was calling to me, like something infernal. Fintan, lad, come out and die!

He must of seen the look I give him because he shrugged a bit.

Of course I was not well in myself, he said. Not quite a whole man, let's say. Anyroad, I ask you, lad, could a guilty fella conjure up a landscape more penitential than this one?

I really wished he wouldn't ask me. Because I didn't know what he was on about. And then I saw he wasn't really asking me at all, he was just gobbing on. Calling me Jaxie like he knew me all his life.

Tiny, he said. That's how I felt. Just a speck. And so terribly alone, as if I were a man in a space fillum. I would walk myself to the edge and no further. I didn't trust the salt, the crust, you see. I was afraid I'd come out here and sink to the neck, and there'd be no one for a thousand miles to hear me crying out. Dear God, can you imagine?

I could, I really could, but it give me the yips to think about it. I wondered how he was still alive, this old prick, letting himself think shit like this.

But that was early days, lad. Now I see it clear. And it's a rare and beautiful place, don't you think? With a memory. Sometimes I think perhaps it's all memory. Here, look at this.

He pointed at a line of emu tracks and scratches and dents left by roos and goats.

Everything that ever happened here is still present now. In the crust, underneath, in the vapours. These days I look out there and it says to me: Here I am, son, still here. I was here before the likes of you and yours were born. Before you even drew breath, I am.

Well, I said. That just doesn't make any sense to me. There's nothing here but us. There's no one talking but you. Jesus, how would anyone get a bloody word in edgeways?

And the old man give off a wheezy laugh and slapped me arm in a way made me step back a bit.

Aw, he said. The cheek of him!

Just saying, I said. And he smiled and scratched his whiskers a sec.

Yes, Jaxie, it's a grand place for a fella to go off his head in.

But here's the joke of it, my friend. If I had the chance to leave this place now, I'm not sure I would.

We looked out east where the far shore was just a red ripple. And when I turned to go because enough was enough I caught a look at that mob of rocks standing up south of us. He must of saw me hesitate.

First time I saw those stones, lad, I thought they were people.

Me too, I thought, but I was buggered if I was saying so.

Got the shock of the ages, Jaxie. I was lonely as I ever was in my life, and the sight of them – well, it was like being struck by lightning. For a moment or two I was overjoyed, you know, as if here was company at last, maybe even deliverance. And then I thought, Oh God, here they come. This is it, the end – they've sent a veritable army to see me off. What a gobshite, eh boy? The arrogance of the old Fintan MacGillis! As if Rome would need a battalion to extinguish the likes of me.

I didn't say nothing to that. Plain fact is I wasn't following at all.

But now, he said, when I catch a glimpse of them out there, those stones, there's a certain reassurance in them. They're company in their way.

So you like it here, I said.

Oh, I've come to terms. After my own fashion.

But you're a prisoner.

Well, not exactly.

Why don't you leave then? No one to stop you.

Have you seen what's out there, lad? I crossed the lake once, from curiosity and desperation. Beyond the farther shore it's desert, you know. A man'd be walking into fire, no less. There was a time in the early days I hauled myself west to the highway, and nearly died of it. Sat down in the shade at the roadside and thought, How will I account for myself, what will I say to whoever comes along? I've no papers, no passport, no money, no real idea where I am, even. Besides, I'm too old for running away, Jaxie. Where would I go? At home there's no one left who'll have me. And out here I'm an alien.

How d'you mean?

A stranger, boy, an exile. I'm lost to my own – I have nobody.

But the people who come with food?

Ah. Well, now.

They're family?

Well, once I might have thought so. But no, what they bring is not so much solicitude as sustenance. Not to mention surveillance.

So they're cops. And this is what, witness protection?

The old man looked at me and smiled. Well, lad, nobody's ever put it that way, but you're not so far from the mark.

I don't get it.

Only out here it's the perpetrator who's witness to his own deeds.

Say that in English.

Well, he said. In plain terms, this is protection for the guilty.

You mean you?

Aye. And them, the same. Only for them it's me who's the awkward problem, because of what I know as much as what I've done.

Jesus, I said. Don't tell me.

Believe me, boy, I have not the slightest intention.

I thought about this a moment. But I had too many half-baked ideas going through me head to get anywhere with it.

They make you wear a GPS tracker?

No, he said. Nothing like that.

There people who come —

It's just the one fella.

When he comes out here, how long's he stay?

Oh, he never stays, never can, never will.

So he's not a mate then.

He's doing his job, Jaxie. He brings me supplies and offers me a certain comfort and I send him away unrequited.

Whoa, I said. I didn't like the sound of that.

He has to offer the sacrament of Reconciliation, lad. That's his job.

What?

It's what we do.

We?

I take it you're not a Catholic, then?

No, I said stepping even further away from him without thinking about it. I don't go in for shit like that.

Yes, I forgot: you're the wild colonial boy.

And it was like I seen him for the first time. Fuck me, I'd been watching him a whole night and day trying to figure the old prick out and it was only now I copped on to what he was.

You said something about your mum, I said.

She's passed, poor darling.

But she sent you somewhere. You said she sent you off.

Oh, he said. School. And then the seminary after it.

Seminary.

Do you not know the word?

I turned right there and then and headed back for the shore. I know what it fucking means, I said over me shoulder.

Jaxie!

I ran for a bit. Right into the setting sun. But the salt surface was iffy and I had no puff in me. So I settled for walking hard as I could for the shepherd's hut and all me stuff. He kept calling and yelling behind me but I wasn't having any of it. I couldn't fucking believe I'd walked into this setup like a retard. I was that angry with meself I could of bitten off me own face in the mirror.

First thing I grabbed when I got back was the Browning. Then the clip. After that the waterjug and me pack with the salt and the rest of the ammo in it. I had to make sure everything was still inside, I couldn't go back into the bush without them boxes of shells, but by the time I had me ducks in a row the old man was in the yard.

I jacked a round up the spout and come out the doorway with me gear on and the barrel pointed his way. He pulled up short with his specs all crooked and put his hands up like some gumby in the movies. But even with a gun levelled at him he didn't stop talking.

Don't go, lad. You've got ahold of the wrong idea.

You're one of them priests aren't you?

A priest, yes. But it's not what you think.

They're fucking hiding you here.

I can't deny it. But it's not for what you may be thinking.

For what then?

Lad, I just can't tell you.

Not even if I blow your foot off?

Jaxie, please, lad. I'm not like you. I'm not a brave man.

Just tell me,

It's not possible. I can't.

You can't even fucking say it can you? Jesus Christ, I could kill you right now.

Aye, you could, Jaxie. I see it.

There's mineshafts all out here, I said. No bastard would ever find you.

True enough. But you'd be making a grievous mistake.

Doing the world a bloody favour more like.

Perhaps. But not yourself. Believe me, lad, there's some mistakes you don't come back from.

You're fucking scum.

I am that.

Fucking hell, how do you even live with yourself?

His specs hung off one ear by now. And in the end the old bastard was shaking so much they peeled off him altogether and fell to the dirt.

How indeed, was all he said.

And the thing is I knew I was never gunna shoot Fintan MacGillis. But the way his legs got the wobbles it looked to me he wasn't so sure. He started sucking in breath and whispering shit and I felt fully ashamed of both of us.

Jesus, I said. Pick up your glasses. I'm not gunna shoot you.

The old prick was halfway to blubbing when I thumbed the mag off and eased the shell out and hung the rifle over me shoulder. It took two goes for him to get his specs back on his face and then he couldn't even look at me when he said thank you.

I'm off, I said.

It'll be dark soon.

I can live with it.

Then take the bedroll, he said. I have no need of it.

I can't carry it.

Well, you're welcome to come back for it.

I don't think so.

Did you take meat?

No, I said. I'm not a thief.

Well, do take some. Please. I'll get you a bag.

I stood out in the yard while he went inside. The sun was on the ridge already and a couple of butcherbirds were doing their sorry-sounding call. And that's when I thought of his knives and the steel. All I had was the poxy little butterknife.

When I come in the doorway the old priest jerked back from the meatsafe like I was about to clout him. He had a tin plate full of goat in his hands and an empty flourbag was out on the table. He'd had enough time in there to get his shotgun and a coupla shells together but he hadn't gone for them.

Just tell me, I said. I won't shoot you for it.

I'm not a rapist, the old man said. I am not a paedophile.

But you're something.

I am.

When you looked at Fintan MacGillis he could have been anything, a science teacher maybe. Or a bloke who sniffs bicycle seats. I didn't know what to believe.

So what's reconciliation? I said. I thought that was for Abos.

A sacrament, said Fintan MacGillis. It's what we used to call Confession.

But you won't do it?

He shook his head.

Fuck, I don't get you people.

Well, Jaxie. That's two of us.

Pedos lie all the time.

I believe so.

If you was a fiddler you'd probably lie about it.

I imagine so. Yes.

He started dumping the whole plate's worth into the bag and I told him I wasn't wanting to take all his meat so he pulled out a few chops and set them back on the plate and wound up the bag. His hands shook and he was clumsy with it so it still felt like I was robbing him. I didn't enjoy the feeling. But the whole scene was starting to make me want to yack so I took the bag and told him goodbye. Then I went out to the tank and filled me jug and he come and stood close enough to give me the creeps.

I wish you'd stay, he said. Really, I do.

Yeah, I thought. I'll bloody bet you do. But I didn't say it. I told him thanks for the food and picked up me waterjug and got going.

I didn't get far before dark. There was no way I was going to even make it back down the lake and to the salmon gums without having to feel me way there like a blind bastard. So I walked straight out behind the shepherd's hut and hauled up into the stony terraces where the gimlets and bluebush were thick enough to hide me. And while it was just light enough to see I found a soft scrape under a kurrajong and got meself settled for the night.

I didn't light a fire. And I was pretty rooted but I didn't sleep right off. I was still stirred up from things back there. I'd never pointed a firearm at a human being before. It's a fucking low thing to do if you're not scared for your life. And there was still this tingling in me legs and arms like something electric, like every bit of me knew what I done and was horrifed.

For a long time I wondered what woulda happened if I went ahead and shot Fintan MacGillis. All the big talk about mineshafts. When the closest diggings were a whole day's walk away. How did I figure I was gunna carry a dead body all that distance? Chop him up and cart him in three trips, push his carcase cross-country in that wheelbarrow?

Thing is, the old dude had only been decent to me. He give me food and water. Could be that was all to soften me up so he could get his priesty hands on me but the worst thing he done was talk me ear off. So I was a bit disgusted about waving a gun in his face. Even if he was a pervert it couldn't be right to just go ahead and kill him.

Then I got to wondering, if he wasn't a pedo like he said, what could they be hiding him for, what would be the use? Jesus, two days ago this country was lonely as Mars, now it felt crowded as a city.

So I sat up for ages. I could see the lake pretty good and I could watch the tiny light in the hut. There was a fingernail moon for a while but it went down behind me. Pretty late the hut light went out and there was nothing but the glow of the salt.

It was warmer out that night. The wind come round to the north and the air was kind of sticky. Everything was quiet, so quiet you could hear a kind of background hum. Like everything was asleep but the world was still running, giving off a noise you can't be sure you're really hearing. Like them bees last year in the lightning tree. The burr they made, it was so low and deep down I didn't even know I was hearing it at first.

It was about Anzac Day I reckon, when we noticed the swarm. There's a tree got split by lightning in a storm once and the bees found it and moved in, and after a few weeks the whole yard smelled of honey. It was only then we started to hear them, and for a while it was all Mum would talk about. She said the smell was divine but she worried about bees coming in the house. It wasn't that she was allergic but she said bees didn't belong inside. Said maybe something should be done. Which meant something should be done by me or the Cap. Wankbag ignored her. Didn't wanna know.

But I was into the bees. She was right about the smell, it was like someone baking every day. And when you got up close to the hive you could feel the heat of them in the tree trunk and the drone was like a chiller room running, I could hear it from me bedroom. Every night at tea Mum says those bees are still there, love, we should do something. But we just eat our chops and watch the telly. Then maybe she rung him at work or something, nagged him so hard he had a gutful. If she did it's a wonder she didn't cop a flogging. But something must of happened because one night the old man comes home from work with a jerry can. Goes straight out the back before tea. And when he come in his arms were stung to fuck and all his fingers were fatter than the sausages on his plate, but he et and watched the news like it was just another night of Happy Families. Mum got her long face on and said nothing. When tea was finished I went out for a look and Mum come out behind me. We just give each other a glance and went in to do the dishes. Wankbag was still at the table pretending to watch the telly. You could see he was waiting for one of us to pipe up about the oily diesel stink and the million crawling bees on the back lawn but we knew better than that, Mum and me. That night in bed I thought I heard that bee hum still going but it was just how angry I was. Some nights there was so much feeling in me head I was glad it couldn't get out. Christ, you could burn a skyscraper down with what's in me. Anyway I spose I dropped off laying there in the powdery dirt under the kurrajong tree listening to that faraway hum, thinking about bees.

I woke up a long time before dawn. Saw the stars through the branches. And remembered how once I saw the moons of Jupiter through the binoculars. A teacher said you could but to me that sounded like typical bullshit. Anyway I tried it and bugger me it was true. I found the Beehive Cluster too. That teacher had a telescope. And he said one day I could look through it but I was always on detention and soon he moved on. After that I wanted a telescope pretty bad but there was no way. Still, it was cool seeing stuff through binocs. A coupla times me and Lee climbed up on the shed roof at night. We looked at Orion's Belt and the Milky Way and that was some stoner shit to see.

The first time you really get the sky, when you see that the moons and planets are places, it nearly takes the top of your head off. Heavenly bodies. The stars, you know, they're pretty to see but it's the idea of them really out there, living and dying, that's even more killer. After a rugged day I guess it's a nice thing to close your eyes on, thinking of that. So I wriggled down into the dirt a bit, felt meself tipping back to sleep.

But then I sat up cold and awake.

The binoculars.

I felt round me neck. I groped in the backpack. But I already knew they wouldn't be there. I knew exactly where they were. Bloody things, I'd left them on the old man's table.

I wanted to up stumps and go get them glasses straight away. But I figured this time of night that was a good way to get me head blown off. So I sat up till I could feel the first grey light and then I got me clobber together and traipsed back down to the lake.

Before I even saw the hut I smelt his fire. I come down through the saltbush and the wattles and followed the track in and there he was, sat by the flames. When he saw me I pulled up and give a wave but he went inside. I wondered if he'd come back out with the .410 but it was only another pannikin he had in his hand when he showed again, and by the time I got there he had it steaming full and waiting for me.

Morning, he said.

G'day, I told him.

Those binoculars, he said. They're in on the table.

I just nodded. I shrugged off all me kit and sat on the milk crate he put out.

Here's to ye, he said, holding up his own pannikin.

Yeah, I said. Ta.

It was quiet with us a minute. Like we was both embarrassed. Then he piped up and said he'd make damper but I told him I still had the meat he give me yesterday, so we grilled it on an old fridge rack over the coals. It was more than we could eat right there and then and I offered to put the rest in the meatsafe but he told me to keep it for the hike back. I wrapped it in the flourbag and shoved it in me pack. The whole time he stayed quiet. I figured I'd put the wind up him yesterday and I probably should say something about it but I couldn't get started.

There was a burr in me sock so I took the boot off and then the sock. And it felt so good to have me foot free in the air I took the other one off as well and squished me toes in the warm dirt. It was nice there in the morning sun. With the smoke and the steamy tea and the taste of fat and sugar staying on in me mouth. I told meself in a sec I was gunna go in and get them binocs. Then pull all me crap on and get going.

You ever seen a dead body? I asked him. And I dunno why I did. Except I was comfy there and putting off leaving. And maybe to show him no hard feelings.

Fintan didn't look up from the fire. He hoiked his dregs over one shoulder.

Aye, he said. I've seen the dead.

It's awful.

Yes, every time.

You think there's people you wouldn't mind seeing dead, I heard meself say. But when you see it.

Aye, it's a horror.

I haven't killed anybody, I told him. I know you think I did. But I haven't.

It's a good thing you left those binoculars, he said. You'll be needing some stores.

Nah, I'm orright.

You have tea and sugar?

I shook me head.

Flour? Paraffin? Soap? Vegetables?

I'll get by.

With a fecking butterknife, now?

I sat back then. And he give me a quick glance and pushed his specs up his nose.

You went through my stuff?

I did. And I'm not sorry for it. How long do you think you can live out here on a dozen bullets and ten pounds of salt?

I'm not here forever. Not eight years, that's for sure. This is temporary.

This is the month of May, Jaxie. On what you have, you won't see June.

I didn't like the way the old man was talking. And he still seemed to think I was planning to set up permanent. But it hit something touchy when he said I wouldn't make it till June because I planned to be close enough to Lee by then to text her and get us out.

Well, I said. I'm not gunna sit on me arse and start talking to meself. I've got somewhere to get to.

From here? Afoot?

I can do it. But it won't be all on foot.

Good God, son, where's close enough you can even entertain the notion?

Mount Magnet, I said.

Ah, he said. It's a place, then? I had Magnet figured for a horse.

I sat there with this awful empty feeling because in two seconds I'd told him everything. Christ, even Lee didn't know what me plans were and I'd blabbed them to the first person I met. But then it sunk in that Fintan MacGillis didn't even know where Magnet was.

I only need a few weeks, I said.

I see.

So I'm orright.

Rightso, he said poking up the fire again. But think on this, Jaxie. What kind of shape d'you want to be in when you get there?

I shrugged. Who cares? What's it matter?

You're staying on Mount Magnet?

It's a town, not a mountain.

You're safe there, then? You'll stay?

Fuck no. We're outta there.

So you're meeting someone?

You don't need to know any more than that, I said, wild at him and me both.

Well, you and this person you're running away with —

Just shut up about that.

Even if she's not a girl – and I'll bet a year's tea and flour she is – she'll not likely get far with a fella too starved and weak to move quickly, and too dirty-looking to pass as a civilized individual. You'll arrive looking like the Wild Man of Borneo. Have you thought of that, now?

I tell you, I could have punched the sneaky old prick in the throat. But I didn't. And it wasn't because I'm such a good bloke I wouldn't knock an old-age pensioner on his arse when he deserved it. It was what he said. How I'd be after a few more weeks of living out there on me own, how I'd look by then. What it'd be like trying to hitch a lift on the highway. What Lee'd make of me turning up looking rough and stinking like a bushpig. When I got there we might only have a moment or two and she'd have to make her mind up right there and then. Course I always believed in me heart she'd come with me. But what if I didn't seem like me anymore, what if I looked scary and feral, what if she suddenly wasn't sure? Would you go on the road with some mad-eyed cunt with shit in his hair and blood up his arms?

I dug me toes in the dirt and bit on the tin cup. And Fintan MacGillis, the bastard, he felt me thinking, it was like he saw right into me.

Lad, he said. All I'm saying is, don't you want to give yourself the best possible chance?

And that was what done it. How I came to stay. I didn't decide right that minute but slowly, while we sat there talking and had another brew. He wasn't even asking me to stop with him anymore, he was offering to give me all these supplies to keep me going, stuff I knew I was gunna have to hump back out to the diggings in stages. It'd take me days if I took half of what he reckoned I needed. I'd be wearing meself out carting cans and bags and drums when I could use those same days hunting from here and working on me plan. Except for salt I had no way of keeping meat at the prospector's shack. And I'd be much closer to the highway back there, more likely to have people come sniffing about. Here, with the water trap, you didn't need to hunt so hard. A box and a half of shells would go a lot further. And there'd be two of us to keep a look out, two sets of hands to get stuff done with. I still wasn't sure about the old priest but I knew he was right.

So I come straight out with it. Said if he didn't mind I'd stay after all. See how it went. He looked so happy I couldn't hardly stand it. And he gobbed on so much he didn't even hear me reasons why.

It was only today I saw he might have made sure them bloody binoculars stayed behind. I know he always hoped I'd stop and keep him company. He just didn't know what that was gunna cost him.

Thing is I still had me doubts.

I was the old man's guest and so I knew I probably wasn't the one should be dishing out rules, but I told him from the start I was only camping at his place. Outside. I was gunna keep all my stuff separate and that meant having me own rifle close. Also it had to be clear I was only there for a bit. And there was no way I was ever sleeping under the same roof as him. No offence, I said, but I'm not taking any chances. And he said yes, yes, of course and by all means. Though he said I shouldn't get paranoid and I told him straight up I wasn't the druggy type. And for some reason he thought that was funny, the dozy old knob.

Anyway we figured it out more or less. I set meself up just

back from his clearing in a clump of gimlets. It was somewhere he could see me and I could see him, fair's fair. He lent me a piece of heavy tarp and I strung it up for shade and in case it rained, but it never did while I was there. I had the swag he give me with a sheet and blanket and even a pillow. And a coupla milk crates and a plastic box with a lid to keep the crawlers out. There was a torch in the hut but not many batteries so he give me some candles and a pineapple tin he cut down for a reflector and windbreak. I didn't need any cooking irons because we figured it was best to eat together, less waste. I could go me own way during the day though we should tell each other what we was up to so there was no accidents with guns. For a safety signal I had that shithawk screech to call down on him so he knew it was me coming, and in the end all he had for an answer was singing The Wild Colonial Boy which is a fucking joke, I know, but we reckoned it'd probably work. Anyone else singing for no reason it'd look suss, but him being Irish that wouldn't count.

Hard to say if we was neighbours now or housemates. Probably neither one. He said we were friends but I said if he ever tried anything friendly on me I'd shoot his cock off. Still, we had to trust each other somehow so I told him I believed he wasn't a pedo, even if in me guts I wasn't so sure. And he said he was certain and sanguine I wasn't a murderer but I expect he wasn't rock solid on that neither. Truth is, it suited me to keep him wondering.

And it sort of worked, our arrangement. Before I couldna seen the sense in it. But two of us getting meat and wood, two of us keeping a look out, it was more efficient than one bloke faffing about on his own. And it wasn't we had anything in common exactly but we was another human to talk to. Though there was a rule about gobbing off as well. We would never say nothing about each other to anyone else. Both of us swore on that. What happened at the hut stayed at the hut. And that meant it was safer we didn't know much worth telling.

So I didn't say I was from Monkton. But it wouldn't of mattered, the old bugger didn't know where he was, he didn't know Monkton from Meekatharra or Melbourne. It was like the priests brung him here in a fucking spud sack. He didn't know shit about Australia or anything in it but he copped on quick and you had to be careful what you let slip. I guess we was both pretty cagey at first. Then it was easy to be careful, like second nature. Fintan said it was just good manners. He called it observing the rule. He had this way of talking that was fairly safe because what he said usually meant nothing much anyway. It was all blardy fucking blah, me boy, blardy fucking blah.

First few days we done a stocktake, he called it. Pulled all the shit off his shelves and out of his drums and counted it up. He figured if it didn't rain too much and the goats stayed thirsty the two of us could last well into the new year. When I told him it wouldn't be two of us still here in the new year he give me the deaf treatment but I knew he heard me.

It was two whole days before he give me a knife he had spare. It was an old boner, a Dexter with a wood handle and a fairish edge, and when I got it on a stone for half an hour it come up way better than fair. I spose that was when I knew he trusted me.

I could of killed him at a distance with the Browning, done it any time of day. But most people're more scared of getting cut than shot. What's worse than the idea of having your throat slashed while you're asleep in your bed? So a bloke with a good knife on him, that's someone you gotta trust day and night, and there I was, camped outside his door, with him hard of hearing and me young and quick and dangerous. Yeah, I could of messed him up with the old butterknife I arrived with but he knew as good as me that Dexter would rip a man's throat open in a second. Maybe I'm making too big a thing out of it. Just seemed to me when he give me that boning knife it sealed the deal between us.

There was always jobs to do at Fintan's place. That was no odds to me, I'm not the lazy type. We oiled the mill best we could. To keep the water up to the trough and because the squeaks and clangs give me the shits even if he couldn't hardly hear them. And there was wiring on the fence to twitch back after every madarse billy got himself snookered. For a bloke Fintan was pretty big on the cleaning and washing. He give me a toothbrush I didn't even ask for. All that got on my tits at first but I got used to it. And he taught me how to cook damper and johnnycakes and whatnot. I always did more than me fair share carting firewood because he was old and gimpy. And a coupla times I went back into the ridge country and popped a roo to give us a break from goat. Fintan loved a bit of roo. He

boiled the tails up nice for a stew. A few times I frenched him
out a rack or two to do in the oven but mostly he liked to fry
up a fillet with pepper and a tomato. Said it reminded him of
beefsteak lunches at the Shelbourne, which is a pub in Ireland.
He said you wouldn't even know it was kangaroo. And I told
him there's plenty of meat tastes like beef when you need it to.

The job I really hated was emptying the shitcan. Fintan said
it used to be once a week on his own but with the both of us
there it was something needed doing every third day and it was
a cunt of a mission. His setup was really just a thunderbox with
a drum you pulled out when it was half full and could still be
carried. You had to hoist it onto the barrow and make sure you
didn't wait till it was too full or you'd tip turds everywhere on
your trip to the junkyard. Jesus, that was a long walk. The flies
sucking at you and rubbing their poopy feet up and down on
you. Then you'd be chipping at the stony ground with the mattock and shovel and when the hole was dug you'd gag your ring
out pouring it all in. Soup Day, Fintan called it. Sometimes I
shat out in the wildywoods just to put off Soup Day one more
morning. Fintan said he would of done the same only he was
too old to get down and squat. Said he'd rather smell it every
third day than fall in it every morning.

Most nights we sat by the outside fire. He read a lot, Fintan
MacGillis. The same books over and over. And he saved an
hour or two to do it in the daylight so as not to waste kero or
candles. But he knew some stuff by heart too. Poems and bits
of the Bible and that and he said them to me pretty often by
the fire after dark. At first I thought it was just to show off how

much stuff he knew but then I saw it was because he was lonely, it was like he said these words up against the dark, like he'd been doing it before I come along and maybe even before he got himself into whatever fuckup put him there.

He was from Ireland where it's green and rainy and people believe in fairies. He said the Irish don't believe in the church anymore and they had a right not to, but they still believe in the little people and the Eeyou. I never did figure out what the Eeyou is. And I think fairy talk is bollocks but he reckoned people had it deep in their bones and he wondered if maybe there wasn't something to it after all, and not just in Ireland. People feel things you can't always see, he said. And I got to admit to meself there's a bit of truth in that because sometimes I know when I'm being watched. And there's times I know when someone's coming, though it's only if I know them. Maybe that's what Fintan was barking on about when I first met him, that some of us still got the animal in us.

This is what I want to talk about with Lee when I see her. One of the things anyway. Because I know she gets shit like that. She's got this cattle dog look sometimes. She's up and going before you've made your move, she feels your mind getting there before you decide. And I guess that sounds like bullshit to most people but I reckon there's something in it. I've had time to think it out. Not as long as the old man but time enough now.

Fintan said he thought people were no more stupid believing in fairies than believing in the church. And even if I agreed with him, talk like that sounded pretty sour coming from a priest. But he had the shits with them blokes, that was clear.

One afternoon I asked him about Confession, why he wouldn't do it if it was such a big deal. I spose it bothered me. Like, you are something or you aren't something, you should shit or get off the pot. And I really thought he'd laugh at me for saying that but he took it serious. It made him chew on his plastic teeth.

That fella, he said, the one who comes here. It's not as if he mourns the state of my soul, you know. You see, Jaxie, securing a confession would advance his own prospects. There are powers and principalities to appease, forces to curry favour with. The whole point of having me here is to make certain I confess to nobody else.

And he lost me there but I could see his heart wasn't in the priest game anymore. I asked him did he still believe in God. He said he wasn't sure, not if God was the peevish schoolmaster he was raised on. But he thought about it day and night. How to believe, what to believe. Truth is I felt sorry for him. Out there at the edge of the lake, a lake with no water in it, he was just making do. He wasn't even thinking of moving on. It wasn't just them who had him parked in the middle of nowhere. He had himself surrounded. No future, nothing to hope for, nothing rock solid to hang onto. He had no family anymore and no friends. That was where we were the same, me and him. But I've got someone to love, someone to go to and he knew it. It was like the less I said about her the more he knew it. I never once told him about getting Lee to Darwin and maybe Queensland but plenty of times he said I had me whole life ahead of me and he was envious.

Jaxie Clackton, he said, I stand in awe of you.

He was probably half taking the piss but sometimes I reckon he wished he was me. And I spose that was fair enough. He was right to.

Pretty soon I lost count of the days. But I knew from the moon when a month was up. Mostly we got along alright, me and Fintan, though it wasn't easy. Some days that deaf old bastard really got on me fillings. Mainly because he wouldn't shut up. It was like he just couldn't. Didn't matter if I was round or not, he talked to himself day and night. Sometimes if I give him the silent treatment he'd cop on and see he was giving me the shits but most of the time he didn't even notice. And maybe it's a priesty thing but I wouldna been there a week before he started bossing me round like I worked for him, like I was his nephew staying over for the holidays, and a coupla times I had to tell him to go and get himself fucked. Like, who did he think he was? Standing round in his poofy hat like the

Sheriff of Pedo Creek. Then he got all pursy and red and said I was an uncultured ingrate. I said he was a knobjob and he called me a juvenile delinquent. But he never pulled a gun on me. And he never flogged me. So I figured I could put up with his stupid nonsense.

There was one day I wondered if I'd been out in the bush on me own too long. If I was halfway tapped like Fintan. It was late and I was coming in from the ridge country north with a field-dressed euro on me back and feeling pretty decent. I stopped to rest a sec and take a sip and when I put down that little roo and sat on the stony shelf beside him the world went quiet. It was like the birds and insects suddenly held their breath, the sheoaks left off their windy sighing and all I could hear was me own breath. And for a moment it was like some creature, some beast was about to come pushing and snorting through the scrub. The feeling was so strong I had hairs up and I put a shell in the spout of the .243 and got ready, looking every which way but seeing only rocks and mulga. I was burred up for action, for ages. It was the only time in all those months I was ever scared in the wildywoods. I took a knee and scoped an arc. Even thumbed the safety off. But nothing turned up.

Except I thought I heard something. Like a motor. A vehicle changing gear. But that couldn't be. There wasn't any tracks up that way. I figured maybe it was a jet. But no plane makes that down-changing sound. I sat and listened a good while. And knew I was just spooking meself because the birds started up again. And I never heard another thing.

So I guess another month went by. And we had our chores and routines, the stuff we liked and the things that browned us off. Fintan reckoned we was the original odd couple, a veritable David and Jonathan he said, like they was some chill dudes.

Early on he give me some goo to put on me puffy eye. Offered to do it himself but I said let me do it myself. So he give me the ointment and the sticky plaster and I stuck it up like that for a week and it come down to normal.

Left a nice old scar, but. Saw it in Fintan's shaving mirror. It didn't look real lovely, still doesn't but there's nothing I can do about it. The old man said I shoulda let him stitch it but I wouldn't let him that close back then. He never come out and asked me how I got it but he wasn't stupid, he had a pretty good idea.

The only time I ever let Fintan touch me was months in. I wanted me head shaved and he was the one with the razor. I got half of it done meself before he said here, let me finish that properly. But it took forever for him to get it done. That blade shook in his hand. Because I did warn him. He knew I didn't want handling by any man. And I couldn't tell if he was nervous or had the hots. He said for pity's sake, lad, stop your wriggling. Lee says I'm twitchy as a pound dog. So it wasn't the quickest haircut I ever got. Still, far as I can tell Fintan did a decent job, though he said it was a shame to make meself look like a convict, even for love, even for my Joan of Arc.

And it took me a minute or two to cop on but when I did it fucking set me off, put a wasp up me clacker that did. The chick in the movie, the one in the fire gutsing it out like all them kings and soldiers and flames and dirty laughing bastards couldn't break her.

Even for love he says. Even for a baldy-head girl like Lee is what he means. Well screw you I thought, you said you never looked at me phone that time or any other time I got suss about it. But how the hell else you gunna know who and what she looks like?

By now there probably wasn't a bee's pube of battery left any- way, I didn't even check anymore, didn't dare in case I needed that last ray of power later on, and now the idea of it being pissed away. By Fintan fucking MacGillis. While I'm out there hunting up a feed. Him like a dirty bush cat going through me stuff, his paws and his priesty eyes all over her. Christ, was I wild.

But I never touched the cunt. It was like I was there in me own fire. And I had control.

I stood up a mo. Rubbed me scabby bald head. Brushed all the fuzz off me arms and chest. Then I went straight up me camp and dug the thing out, saw it was dead and gone. I stashed it in a hollow log where not him or any other shithead could get at it. Battery or no battery I couldn't come at the idea of people touching that phone now.

I spose I took a minute or two to kick the skin off some poor tree minding its own beeswax. And then I went back down and give the old dude a red hot mouthful. Told him he had no fucking right, the filthy perv. And he swore he never once touched the thing but I knew he was lying. I told him I had a bloody gutful. Said he had no self-control, he was like a fucking child, said he bloody disgusted me. Then he give me the puppy eyes and when that didn't work he did the shaky lip thing and I said I should break all his fucking fingers but I wouldn't because then I'd have to do all his bloody jobs as well as mine. Then I ran out of things to say and he went in and layed on his bed and had a bit of a sook.

So that was me day rooted. I took the Browning and fucked off. I could of left for good that time. And true I got close. For a while out in the ridge country I thought of coming back for me gear and pissing off there and then. But I chilled a bit. Just from walking really. There was birds to see, finches and quail, things to take me mind off him.

And in the afternoon I sprung a big red roo. Truth be told, we sprung each other. He looked at me like he couldn't believe I existed, like me being there just wasn't right. I shot him as he turned to go and he spun round like he was dancing and when he went down I felt kind of sick.

For a few minutes I didn't go near that buck. I wasn't taking any chances getting me guts ripped open if it wasn't properly dead. That was part of it. But also there was this sad feeling, something I never got when I took me turn to off a goat down in the mill yard. Fact is I wasn't real keen to get over and see what I done. A goat's got eyes make it pretty easy to kill. Them flat snaky pupils, they stop you feeling like a prick for doing what has to be done. But a roo's got a big round cow eye and it makes everything different. Same with dogs and cats. I can't never kill another one of them, not even for mercy.

Mrs Mahood come over one day when Mum first got crook. We thought it was like a sick visit, but not even close. Said she had a mob of kittens nobody wanted and she didn't have the heart to deal with them herself, would Mr Clackton see to it for her. Seeing as how he wasn't so particular. Mum kind of froze her off then. Like she was a fucking Mormon. But that night there was a bag of cats outside the back shed. When he got in the Captain said the fuck he would and he left them there. Two days later the old girl come over again and saw the bag still goomfing and meowing all over the path and she cracked the waterworks. Mum was in bed and the Cap was at the shop so it was up to me. She said what kind of person could treat creatures that way? Like wasn't I ashamed?

Well I picked up that wriggling pissy sack and took it out in the street. Heard her clomping along behind me as I went down, kicked her gate open. Right up on her porch I took it, up with the white swans and the flowerpots and all. Bashed them kittens to shit against the verandah rail. Four, five, six times. She made this noise like a strangled crow. Looked at me like I was a fucking monster. Not even a thank you.

Anyway the afternoon I shot that big red roo I faffed round like some old woman putting off the messy bit, the butchering that is. Told meself I was letting the meat set, that I was getting the knife edge back up before I got into it. Shit like that. But I knew I was only stalling.

In the end I stepped over the rocky ground between me and this old buck and saw he was bled out and dead as a rock. But when I squatted down with the Dexter I looked at his big brown eye and saw meself, a reflection of me, a kind of shadow looming out of the sky and I had this mad idea, like there it is, Death, that's me, that's what I am. A few weeks ago a thought like that woulda charged me up but now it was depressing. All the same it didn't stop me trimming him down and dressing him out while he was still warm and flexible. I reckon it took me near on four hours to get him back down to the shepherd's hut and when I was still a long way off old Fintan come out and met me and it was like I'd brung him a present, a peace offering, he was clapping his hands and dancing like a nut. I got a good fire going and we had ourselves a feast and after that things were okay between us again. More or less. I even started sharpening his knives for him to make it up, ground away while he read stuff or said it out from memory.

Like I said, we got along okay most of the time. Except for when we set each other off. Sometimes that was accidental, like one of us'd say something without realizing and it made the other one blow turds and kick the wall. Other times we knew we was digging and niggling and we did it because we was bored or just evil for a minute. And some days it was hard to know if the shit we said was random or if it come out on purpose. Like when I asked him about dead people. Because it wasn't just the once I piped up on that. There was something about the way he talked the first time made me want to try him again. He said I come back to that business like a dog to its vomit.

See, I kept remembering what Auntie Marg said in Moora that day we went down to see Nan dead in her house. She said Nan had a good death. I was only a kid then but it still got me. And now I'd seen three dead people and touched two of them and I didn't need to lay a finger on them to see what they were. The moment you come near, everything in you goes cold. In your arms and legs and teeth you know what you're seeing is horrible. When they're dead the whole of them is wrong. It doesn't have to look like what I saw out there in the shed, it's bad however it happens. And I kept thinking, is a good death just a stupid thing people say? Like what some of them said at Mum's funeral, I'm sorry for your loss, like they were on the fucking telly or something. Because I just didn't see the good in it, all the peaceful merciful bountiful bullshit the padre said about death before he give the nod and the coffin went in.

So it was one morning up the junkpile. I was digging a new hole with the mattock even though it wasn't Soup Day, because we figured it was better if you dug it the day before and didn't have the bucket standing there reeking to the fuckhouse for half an hour while you tried to chip out a dip in the stony dirt. I stood resting a second and saw Fintan looking at them old beds and kero fridges and rolls of barbwire. I didn't even think to be dark on him for standing round while I did the digging, I just had that good death thing on my mind.

You seen dead people, I said.

Yes, he said without even looking my way. Too many. I told you.

You're a priest. I spose you buried them.

Buried? I've seen them pushed into pits with bulldozers, he said.

I didn't know what to say to that. I was standing there with me mouth open.

Seen them stacked and burnt like piles of rubbish.

Jesus. Where?

It doesn't matter. And don't ask.

I took a swing with the mattock and sparks flew off a stone and I straightened up again. I looked at him and thought, well that's the end of that talk. But Fintan lifted his singlet and scratched his guts and kept looking at all the wrecked stuff in the pit.

A hole bigger than this trench, dug with a machine. Full of bodies. And you know something? I sat in the shade of a butter-fly tree and drank tea. It was a grand pot and a lovely tree.

I don't get it.

Well, that's two of us. Because I didn't feel a twinge. And yet when my own dear mother lay dead on her bed I was deranged by it.

You mean you went mad?

Not truly. Though it felt that way. There was no smell, no flies. She went peacefully in her sleep, and there was a turf fire burning in the grate and gentle traffic outside the window. All the same, you're at the scene of a horror you'll never come to terms with. Nice people bring you cocoa and you look at it like it's poison. You think, I'll never eat or drink again.

Which come first?

Whatsay?

What happened first, your mum or the other thing?

Are we not observing the rule today, lad?

I dunno, I said. Is that the same as not observing my phone?

Oh, are we after that again? Have you not a shred of mercy?

I wanted to ask him where he saw this bladed ditch full of bodies. And I didn't know what a butterfly tree was neither. But I bit me lip and got on digging. Because I wasn't in the mood for arguing. Then a minute later I started up again and told him about Auntie Marg and the good death she kept talking about. I told him how that got up me, it didn't seem right any way you looked at it.

Perhaps what she meant to say is your nan had an easy death, he said. Sure enough, it's something to be grateful for. So many hard ways to die.

I know, I said.

I fear you do.

I've seen it.

Yes, lad. I have no doubt. I sense it in you every day.

So if one's easy and the others are hard, then what's she talking about?

Oh, Jaxie, who could say?

I just thought someone like you would know.

And then he give a sort of groan.

I don't know that I do, he said. Everything I once stood for was predicated upon a noble end, the example of a brave, fine, pure death. And by God, half the people I knew and loved went in search of something like it, to emulate it. We were all mad for it. Seems to me we spent half our born days curating our own good deaths. Nowadays that strikes me as absurd and perverse, utterly monstrous. But I'm not a good judge of monsters; I don't know if the idea of a good death repels me now because it's in itself repellent, or because I no longer have the courage to seek such a thing.

I don't know what any of that means, I told him. Can you say it in English?

He pressed his knuckles to his head. For a bloke not doing any digging he looked hard worked already.

Alright, then, he said. You know what a sacrifice is, yes?

The Anzacs.

Whatsay?

When you die for your country, I said.

Oh, he said. I see. Well, yes. For your family, your country, your faith.

You don't believe in that?

That's how I was raised, lad. These are the good deaths. Apparently. But we have something in common, you know, you and I. We recoil before the notion. Every death is a horror, is it not? Every end a cataclysm, an outrage.

Fintan gummed on them plastic teeth of his and kicked the side out of a rusty drum and the old 44 shook but didn't roll.

Those feckers who blow themselves up outside hospitals and markets. The eejits who fly aeroplanes into city buildings. They think they're martyrs, you know. They've studied on it, the business of giving themselves a good death.

That's not a fucking sacrifice. That's murder.

Well, it takes some courage to be a murderer too, you know.

Bullshit, I said. That's sick.

Or a soldier. Or a bureaucrat. Or a priest who tells a million people their deaths are willed by God, the fruit of their obedience, an ornament to their reverence for life.

I spat on me hands, mostly for the chance to look away. Because now I wished I hadn't asked him anything at all. I didn't go for the way he was talking right then. And I hated the eyes on him when he got like that. Eyes of a steer. It made me sick to look at him.

Jaxie, be happy for your nan. An easy death is something to be envied. There's no shame in it. Isn't it what any sane person would wish for, to go quietly in his sleep?

Fuck that, I said. I don't ever wanna die. I'm gunna go down fighting.

Could be it's harder to surrender.

Jesus, listen to you with your arse-about talk. Brave to be a murderer. Harder to surrender. You're all fucking words and no balls.

Oh, pish posh, boy. Are we finished digging this hole yet?

Here, I said, ditching the mattock his way. You fucking finish it.

Down at the lake there were trees up in the sky, all stood on their heads. It was beautiful and funny like he said it was, so at least he was right about one thing. And seeing that made it hard to stay angry at him. It was just a stupid mirage but I stood out there and watched it till I didn't mind it wasn't real.

So we had some blues, me and Fintan. He said we were merely conducting civilized conversation. But sometimes it was like he didn't know how close he was to getting his head stove in. Or maybe he didn't care. Even so, everything was peaceful more or less. Until the wind come round from the north.

III

Out there by the lake the weather was near on the same every day. Of a morning, before dawn, the wind got up from the east. Then by about noon it come round from the south. In this way it was no different to Monkton that time of year. Some people would find that boring but it suited me fine.

But then one morning the easterly didn't show at all. That day was hot and breathless. The air got sticky and the lake stunk like a tadpole puddle. In the middle of the morning a string of emus come in from the salt and stood watching me and Fintan as we twisted out washed sheets and hung them on a wire off the mill tower. They give us this horrified look like what we were doing was some weird ugly shit, what Fintan called crimes against nature. But emus are total goony birds, they always have that shocked look on their faces and they can stand there and stare for hours, the dumb buggers. They just parked out in the samphire and peered at us while we strangled the water out of innocent laundry. And it was funny for a while. Then they got on me tits and I chased them off with a lump of wood. I don't know if I did it from plain shittyness or because there's nothing like seeing an emu run. Thing is, once I saw them off I didn't feel any better. Like I said, the weather was strange. Everything started getting up me. Peevish, the old man said I was. Fucked off more like.

Fintan was a wanker for doing laundry. We had words about it every week. But naturally he always had the most words. And he could spout them in Irish too. Guttersnipe, gobshite, gouger, all that shit. Mostly it was just gobbing off to pass the time and mostly I never give a damn, it was just talk. Sometimes it was fun. And it wasn't so special that day, the stuff he walloped on with, but once we got the sheets hung out I got a mood on. That old restless feeling.

All the time I was at the shepherd's hut it come and went, that itch. Some days I had this feeling I was stuck. Like I'd let meself get comfy. That I was no different to him. I had meat and water and a swag. And I didn't go to sleep worried or get up scared. But the thing is I wasn't going anywhere. And knowing it got me itchy to go.

That was how I was that still, sticky day. I'd seen enough trapped goats by then. Watched them figure out they was caught. And I thought, that's not gunna happen to me. The next time Jaxie Clackton's stuck they'll be nailing him in a box, and you can take that to the bank.

But I was kidding meself totally because I mighta been safe but I was fenced in at the shepherd's hut fair and square. I was kidding meself thinking I was free. The truth of it bubbled up like acid and got me filthy on everything. I knew right then I was gunna run.

Fintan knew me moods good enough by then so that morning after the washing he steered clear of me. I sulked off and hung under me tarp all day, sat there without a shirt and plaited up some rawhide. I got the idea to make a band for the old man's gay hat, give it to him for a goodbye present. And I finished it up late in the arvo but I never did give it to him. I tidied up me crap a bit to make it easier to load when I pulled the pin. Did it sly so he couldn't tell. Let him think I just had the pouts. He wouldn't guess I was getting ready to leave. Tomorrow might work. Day after at the latest.

At sundown I come in by the fire and we et our meat and tomatoes and greens. And I let him give out about Ireland to keep him happy. He went on about some dude called Christy Ring who he swore was a bloke but I wasn't really listening. Me mind was on Lee. And heading north. Getting free. It's funny you know because Fintan used to ask me all the time, like a possum chewing at a live power cord, Jaxie, lad, what is it you want, what is it you're after from life? And I'd say, what does anybody want? And he'd go, most lads only think of sex. And I said speak for yourself.

In the end he wore me down. Always asking. And the answer I give him is still the only one I have. What do I want? Peace. And it actually shut him up. He didn't niggle me about it. It was like he got it straight off. I don't just want quiet neither, I want peace.

I kind of wish we'd talked about that sort of thing this warm evening. Instead of him going on about Christy Ring and me not listening. But I sat there and went away in me head and after a long time I saw he'd talked himself dry and was nodding off. So I kicked the fire in and called it a night.

But when I got to me swag where the sheets were clean and slippery smooth I was too keyed up to sleep. Everything was quiet down the hut and in the bush but I could feel meself listening for something, like I was expecting Fintan to start clanging round down there. Nothing at all was happening but I was waiting, straining to hear.

I thought of them bees at home again. Because once I finally heard them I was always listening for them. And I even caught meself listening for them when I knew they were dead and gone. One time before Wankbag brung the diesel out I went and put me head against that split tree. The sound of it was low and steady like you'd maybe hear on a ship, with the engine deep under the decks right down below the waterline, keeping everything going. The whole world smelt of honey. I wished I could have Lee there with me so we could lean our heads in together and feel the hot sweet breath coming out the black mouth of that tree. And remembering it made me so fucking miserable I could of cried.

And then I couldn't stand to lay there another minute. I got up and pulled on me boots and futzed about finding me tree-hole in the dark and then I dug the phone out of it and got back in me swag and switched it on. Just to look at old stuff from before Christmas, texts and posts and shit. Just to see Lee's face, look into her uneven eyes. And you wouldn't believe it but for a moment the bloody thing lit up, said no service, emergency calls only, and it was like a miracle. But before I could even thumb up a pic the fucker died on me. All I had was that pale blue light burnt into the back of me eyes and it stayed in me like moonlight glowing on inside me head.

Then I knew I didn't even need a lame-arse phone. I had the light of her in me. Had her face right there in front of me. So I stared hard into her eyes, the green one first and then the grey, knowing she'd feel me there in her room, in the dark, up at Magnet. She always got me, Lee, and now I knew she'd get me tonight, laying there in her bed, feel me like a sheet on her so she could pull me up to her chin and be safe. Lee. Lee. Jesus, Lee. I was aching like a hungry animal, glowing like a fucking bushfire and I knew she felt me. There was no bloody way she couldn't. I was a storm on the way. The smell of food, the sound of clean water. There isn't one thing in the world hot and hard as knowing there's someone waiting, coming, pressing, wanting you. Even a priest understands it, I get that now. But that night it was like food falling from the sky.

I got a horn like a lonely rhino just thinking about her. I coulda knocked one out right there and then and be done with it but it woulda felt cheap. So I layed back down aching and after a while I was calm again. Tomorrow I'd tell Fintan I was off. I was charged and ready.

I woke up in the night with a little sweat on. And right away I knew something was off. Different I mean. The moon was already set behind me and the stars had rolled over but whatever had changed so much it woke me up was closer to home than that. First light wasn't so far off but the birds were still asleep. There was no lamp on in the hut and no sound from down that way.

I sat up and got me boots on. Then I put me head against the tree the way Wankbag taught me. He used to say a good sailor could hear surf on a reef in the dark if he pressed himself to the mast and listened up. Now I heard a steady hum. Like the world idling along. And then something else. A hitch in the hum, like a beat missing from it now and then. The unevenness is what I caught. The sound itself was too normal to hear.

And then the salmon gums shivered over me and a warm wind come in from the north. I took me boots off but only to drag me camo strides on. I felt for everything round me in the dark, the binoculars, the rifle and ammo, the waterjug. I pulled me shirt on and yanked the hunting jacket down off a branch.

That sound only come in fits on the wind but it was there alright.

I got me duds on and snatched me kit together.

Once I got a fire going out by the hut I went inside to find the billy. I was slow and quiet but the old man stirred anyway. Christ knows, he couldn't have heard me. And I was fresh washed so he didn't sniff me out neither. But even asleep the old bugger felt me there.

Whoever you are, he said, you should know I have a shotgun.

Don't be fucking wet, I said. I'm standing right next to it.

Jaxie? What are you doing?

Get up, I said. We got a problem.

What're you talking about, boy?

You deaf bastard, you got neighbours.

The light come up while we were sitting out by the fire. The sky started off pink but it was already turning grey again, like a front was on the way. The wind was still in the north and getting up a bit. We grilled some chops and drank a full can of tea. By the time the first sun touched the lake I had me shit sorted. Fintan was all for heading out with me but I wouldn't have it. He was too old and slow, no point pretending he wasn't.

At first he hadn't believed me about that noise. With day here and the trees clattering and the birds going on like shopping ladies you couldn't catch it anymore anyway. But I told him what it was, what it had to be. That was the sound of a generator I heard, a genny running low on petrol. And he looked at me funny and rolled his mouth round like it was a stone I give him to taste. Then he said it didn't really matter, if there was someone north of here they weren't bothering us. I said that was rich coming from a bloke who thought I was the end of days. I said it was better to know who was there than be surprised all of a sudden. He didn't want to agree with that. I could see it wasn't the fact of it he had a problem with, it was just he preferred to pretend everything was alright, that nothing had changed, because he liked how things were now. But in the end he give in to it. A generator close enough to hear, no, that wasn't good. All the same it looked like he was more rattled by the idea of me leaving him than by the thought of some other bastard out there we didn't know. It spooked me how careless he'd got.

How long have you been hearing this? he asked while I filled the waterjug. He was following me round like a little kid.

I dunno, I said. Now I've noticed it I think it coulda been there all along. Only this northerly means it's carrying.

Doesn't make any sense, he said. A breeze comes from that direction periodically. And I've never heard it.

Well, duh. They'd have to be firing Scud missiles before you copped on.

It doesn't seem possible.

What, you think it's fairies?

No need for that, now.

I know there was a salt mine north of here. But that must be thirty kays off. And I was little then.

Oh, dear God, he said, like he was finally getting it.

So how far have you been up that way? I asked.

Oh, I don't know, lad. I walked an hour or two. I saw ruins of an old farm property, but there were no sheep, no cattle, no people. Only wild goats and some broken machinery.

When was this?

Whatsay?

When? When did you go there?

Oh. Well, now. Three years ago, mebbe four?

And there was no one at all?

Abandoned.

I screwed the jug lid down and took it back to where I had me gear layed out under the verandah and he tagged me all the way. And when I pulled the pack on he retied the billy and fiddled with the webbing for me, like he was a strapper at the races. In the end I had to shrug the old bugger off and then I felt bad.

Will you be back, I wonder?

That's the plan, I said.

Well, look at you in your camouflage. A terror to Australia, indeed!

I didn't know what to say to that. It sounded like he was taking the piss but the look on his face give me a flutter, so I just strapped on the .243 and got going.

I worked north along the lake, keeping to whatever ratty bits of mulga I could see round the edge. Now and then I found a few salmon gums and yorkies for cover but there was a lot of patchy red dirt. And rocky shit that made me glad I brung boots and not me Vans. The northerly was up with a coupla points of west in it and that was all I could hear except birds and the sound of me own breath. I was careful with the water and glad the day was grey because it was warm and I was pushing pretty hard.

About midday, just past a big elbow in the lake, I found the stump of an old windmill and some dry pipe and a few bent up sheets of corry iron. There was a long gravelly spur rising up to the west with a coupla overgrown ruts winding along it.

I turned up it till I come to a bigarse straining post and I stopped next to that for a sip. I sat there for a minute or two to rest me feet. Pulled the glasses out to get me bearings and study things.

When you scanned back down the lake to the south it was like looking at a drawing some kid hadn't finished, hadn't got round to sketching the details and didn't even bother colouring in. You'd never know Fintan was down there in his hut. As far as you could see there was no road or roof or mill, no sign of people at all. And it was no different looking north. If there was still a saltworks up there it was too far away even for binoculars. That lake was like its own country.

Angling off from the straining post you could just make out two overgrown firebreaks meeting. And two lines of fucked out spreaders that were mostly down or gone altogether. So I figured this was a boundary corner. In among the whipsticks and suckers, snakes of rusty wire lay on the ground. I found a half buried gate and saw the faint ruts heading northwest. Any numbnuts could see no vehicle come down this way in years. Hell, if you weren't paying attention you'd lose the track completely.

Higher on the range line, out in the west, I caught white blobs moving but that was only goats. It was bare rock up there, like they'd et the place down to nothing. It looked like something off the news, like bloody Afghanistan or something. I couldn't believe anyone was really out this way. Maybe I'd come too far. I figured I'd bail if I didn't see anything soon. Give it half an hour then turn back to the lake.

I pressed on till I found the rusted out shell of an old F100 with buffel grass growing up through it but that was all there was. I was ready to turn back until I come to another track running straight across me path. It was just a set of ruts with the middle weeded up to me shins but it had a fresh run of treads over it and when I saw them I got a real jolt.

The track seemed to go north–south. To the north there was a low rise and I kept on that way, staying in the scrub at the side to leave no prints and so I always had cover to duck into if someone showed. Now that I looked properly, there were two sets of identical treads. One in and one out. I went slow and careful, low as I could.

Just before the rise I got on me belly and crawled to the crest and saw the land dip into a big plain hemmed in all round by ridges and rocky spurs. I glassed it end to end but there was nothing much to see. Though once I got me breath under control I could hear something. There it was. Still faint but clear enough. The sound of a motor. And nothing to match it up with. No buildings or fences or even a windmill. Just salt-bush and low mulga, red dirt and pebbles. I stayed there a long while, straining to see something I knew I should be able to see. No one there, nothing moving, not even a bird. I had the Browning off me shoulder by then. I swapped the glasses for the telescopic sight. And still saw bugger all.

Once I was over that rise and down the other side, the lake was gone behind me. And the further I went the stronger the sound got. The tyre treads were wide and chunky like something off a 4×4. But that engine noise wasn't any kind of vehicle, I knew that already. I followed the treads through the mulga to a big bare patch of dirt where they did a kind of loop on themself.

But this wasn't just a turnaround. It was a clearing. A big patch someone had bladed off with a dozer. The sort you make to build a house and sheds on. There was a kind of windrow at one end, just a nest of dead trees left where the machine had pushed it. All the trunks and limbs were grey and dry and ant-eaten. And all over that scraped ground there were weeds and suckers coming up everywhere, except for one totally bare patch in the middle that didn't look right and I couldn't figure out. And that was it. There was nothing else down there. Just a big clearing in the middle of the mulga. Which freaked me out a bit because the noise of the engine was clear as anything. Not loud, kind of low and light but it felt close by.

So I stayed back for a long time. Didn't even set foot in that clearing. Kept to where there was hardbaked ground underfoot and saltbush and bluebush growing up through it undisturbed. I put a round up the spout. Because I didn't feel safe. Because here was this blank bit of ground making a noise like a four-stroke petrol motor. Invisible. And spooky as shit.

I did this half circle creep round the clearing.

It's so weird to be looking at a sound and not seeing anything. And from this angle it's not one clean note neither. That genny's getting the hiccups. And I know what that means. A dirty carby. Or it's running out of fuel.

Pull out the glasses again. Run them over that clean bit of pindan where nothing's grown back.

Then I catch a shadow. A kind of hard edge. I scoot round

more to the north and the noise is louder. I can even smell it now. And a second later I cop on.

They've buried it. Some cunning bugger's stuck a genny in a box and sunk it in the ground to keep it quiet.

I step out onto that clear stretch and the red dirt's spongy underfoot. I get on me hands and knees and I feel the earth's not right. Too soft. Not natural. Like it's been dug over. And then there it is, an exhaust pipe, just a snout lifted free in a nest of stones someone's put there real careful. You wouldn't see the thing unless you nearly stood on it. It's brilliant. I put me hand over the end and feel the hot breath against me palm. Then I scrape round it and follow it back to something wider, like a car muffler, and pretty soon I find the air intake, just a bit of PVC pipe with a fan down its neck a way. It doesn't take long to find the first flat bit of fridge panel, same shit a chiller room's made of, and when I put me hand down there I can feel the vibration. Then I go and grab a stick and scoot along a way until I scratch up a fuel line. Follow that till I hit something hard and dig down to see the corner of a fuel tank. Can't even guess how big that bugger is. You can bet it won't be anything small.

I straightened up and stood there a minute, me fingertips gone all prickly. Tell the truth I was kind of pumped. Knowing I wasn't just imagining that noise at night. Stoked I was good enough to come up here and sniff this setup out. Whatever the hell it was.

And that's when it dropped on me, plain and hot as daylight. This genny was powering something and whatever that was, it was underground. Other stuff was buried here, something a lot bigger than a petrol motor and a monster fuel tank. And somebody'd gone to a shitload of trouble to hide it.

I walked round in loops for a bit talking to meself like Fintan. Trying to think straight.

This didn't look like any prospecting setup. The ground was dug over but there was no slag or spoil or whatnot. Also no shaft. If you was digging for gold you needed a way to get the stuff out. Unless they covered it while they were gone to keep the find a secret. But what was the power for? Mines have to pump water out but there was no sign of anything like that, no other hoses, no puddles or even any damp patches.

I thought of those survival dudes on YouTube with their bunkers full of food and water and blankets and ammo and everything. Cool setups some of them but those blokes were all nutburgers, the same bug-eyed Yanks yabbering about world government or Donald Trump or some bullshit. There's no shortage of crazy-arse bastards in this country neither but nobody's gunna dig a bomb shelter out here with no water, that's just mental.

And then I got a horrible thought. Like an idea that was really off, totally wrong. I couldn't even tell you where it come from. Except there's shit you see. In movies, online, whatever. I got a creepy cold feeling just thinking it. And it's kind of embarrassing to say it now but for a second or two the picture I got in me head all of a sudden was kids. Women as well. No clothes on. Covered in dirt and shit. In the dark. All tied up in some dungeon thing. Like a sexy pervy outfit some sick cunt's rigged up. To get his jollies. Or make vids to sell to dirty sicko scumbags. Just the thought of that. Under me own feet. People trapped down there in a locked room. Like they could be hearing me walking round and talking to meself up here and they're screaming and calling out for help, poor sods. It was nearly enough to make me yack.

Then something else. Something worse. What if this was what Fintan MacGillis was out here for, why he was so bloody cagey, why he didn't want me coming up this way on me own? Filthy fucking priests been doing shit like this forever, that's not news. And not just them neither. Culty weirdos in America, sicko fathers in Germany and wherever. I seen news on it, old blokes keeping women and kids underground or bricked into basements and everything for their dirty fucking hobbies, holding them down there for years, having babies off of them. And out here who'd ever hear a thing? There was a Chinese crowd busted open north of here a year or two back. End of the world mob. End of days, says Fintan. That's what he asked me. Are you the end of days? And he tells me nothing, never says what he's out here for and I know it's not something on the up and up.

So what is this then? And Fintan, what's he, the caretaker? Fucking hell, he could be the ringleader. Then he's got me foxed through and through. Holy shit.

Pretty soon I went from having an act to getting panicky. I had to do something or I'd twist off completely. So I started poking at the dust with the rifle barrel, spearing the soft dirt all over, spiralling out from the genny and fuel tank till I felt a tunk and knew I'd finally hit metal. Chucked the Browning, pulled off the binocs and got down on me knees and scratched the dirt up like a staffy. And there it was, a steel edge. I scuffed up more dust, found a corner. Christ, it was like a buried truck. No, a shipping container. So I hacked a little trench inwards until I saw a different colour metal. And a hinge. A flat shiny panel. Another hinge. When I cleared it properly I saw it was a door. A lid more like.

All of a sudden I wasn't in such a hurry anymore. I just looked down at that steel hatch. Dusted the latch off. Wondered if I should piss off right now. Like maybe people are right, there's some things you really don't wanna know, stuff you can't wipe clear once you seen it. But if there's people trapped down there in the dark, women and kids desperate, you can't just shovel dirt back on them and walk away. Can you?

So I sucked it up, slipped the latch and lifted the lid.

There was no darkness. It was brighter than day down there. Everything white and jungle green. And the stink, it was like nothing you ever copped in your life. Lights, hoses, white buckets, wires and tinfoil everywhere. A fan turning like it was looking for me. An ally ladder shining right up the chimney hole.

I stuck me head down and called out hullo? But there was no kids or naked women. Just plants the size of men. A whole fucking sea container of hydroponic weed. You never seen so much skunk in your life.

I pulled me head up out of that hole so quick I caught me ear on something, nearly ripped the fucker off by the feel of it, and when I pressed me hand against it there was blood down me arm. I knelt there for a bit too stunned to think or move, me head full of stars again. Then I slapped the lid shut, snapped the latch and kicked dirt back over everything.

I grabbed me rifle and fucked off. Ran like a mad bastard.

Dear God, boy, he said when I come in. Look at the state of you.

I leant the Browning against the wall and saw the barrel was all bunged up with red dirt. The empty waterjug hit the cement floor with a hollow sound. I pulled off the pack and me jacket and he poured me a pannikin. I was blowing so hard I had trouble getting the water down me neck. The hut smelt of meat and ash. There was a pot of something on the stove and the window shutter was propped on the last wedge of afternoon sun.

I'm sorry to say it, lad, but you reek like the last heathen alive.

Well I been going all day, haven't I? Fucking ran most of it.

Of course, he said. Perhaps I'll take myself outside for a breath of fresh air.

And for real Fintan took himself out. Actually stepped round me like I was roadkill. And I nearly bloody cracked it.

Jesus, I yelled through the open window. Are you serious?

No offence intended, he said, stirring up the coals in the fire pit.

You're a fucking tosser, you know that?

I drank another mug of water. Then I chugged down one more. And once I got me wind back I saw me shirt was soaked through and me dacks were so wet you'd think I'd swum a creek in them. And now I was starting to cool off, that slimy feeling got a hold. Sweat and red dust turned to pink paste all over me.

I went out under the verandah and sat on a crate to kick me boots off. Me socks were clammy as frangers. And me legs felt crampy. All I wanted was a feed and a lay down. But the old prick was right, I did need a scrub. Anything to feel better than this.

So what do we know? Fintan asked.

We got a problem, I said, getting up. We need to talk.

Where are you going, then?

I'm off to Maccas, I said. You want me to bring you anything? Happy Meal?

Whatsay?

I'm getting a bloody wash.

And you're taking the rifle?

Like I said, we gotta talk.

Well, take a clean towel at least, he said, all pouty like I was the one being unreasonable.

I snatched it off the wire going past.

You'll feel all the better for it, lad.

Well, I said. You better bloody hope so.

And I did feel like a bit of a knob taking the .243 to the water trough with me but me head was spinning. It was suddenly like I wasn't sure I could trust him. That hydroponic setup. Could he be that deaf? Was it possible he wasn't in on it? A crazy old hermit was like the perfect cover for this sort of shit. And the thing with me phone. Maybe he wasn't lusting on Lee. I didn't even check if he'd been making calls. Except there was no signal. Damn it to buggery, I was all over the place.

So I was glad to see the mill yard empty. Didn't want to be sharing the facilities with any slug-eyed goat. And I stood the Browning up the high end of the trough where it was in reach. Then I climbed in duds and all and fuck me, was it fresh. The trough was slimy and the bore water so hard the soap could barely work up a bubble but it was good to feel the heat and grime come off, and after a minute or two the cold burn smoothed out to something pretty decent.

Then I got this sad feeling. Looking out at the lake. And the clearing. The salmon gums up against the sunset. Because none of it was the same now. Whatever the deal was. Even if old Fintan was as clueless as he was making out I couldn't stay there anymore. True enough I was planning to shoot through only last night, but now the idea of leaving this behind give me a bit of an ache. And I took that out on me duds. I yanked everything off and scrubbed them best I could. Maybe I didn't need to flog them against the trough quite so hard but at least when I come back up to the hut I was calmer.

I hung me bits and shits from the wire out front. The old man had the cookfire burning high. And with all them arms and legs strung up there and the flame light on everything dripping and leaking, the washing line looked like a killing yard, like everything I owned was butchered and gone.

I stood by the fire a minute, just in the towel and nothing else, and Fintan went in the hut and come back with another lame-arse shirt and a pair of shorts so big I had to tie them up with baling twine. There was a stew keeping warm at the edge of the fire. The smell of it was nice. But like something in the past already. And when I was dressed and sitting down the old man filled a plate and passed it over. I went at that gear like a savage.

Your ear's bleeding, he said. Jaxie, what've you done to yourself?

It's nothing.

So what is it we need to talk about? What have you seen that's put half the north wind up you? I've never known you like this, boy. Look at you there with your Orangeman stare. Is it a ghost you've seen? Tell me, now. Get it off your chest.

And now I'd slowed down and got food and water in me I wasn't sure I wanted to say anything at all. I thought of how much fuss and noise it would have took to bring a ship container in on a truck and crane it off and dig a hole the size of a swimming pool in the dirt. That took big machines. It just

didn't seem like the old priest could be that deaf. How does a
bloke not hear a dozer or a digger so close? And for a fella shit-
scared of being sprung he was pretty relaxed about suddenly
finding there's neighbours only half a day's walk away. In a
vehicle, if there was a direct track between this place and that,
if you knew where you were going and what you were doing,
you could do that trip in half an hour. Why else would he be
so bloody cool unless he knew about it all along? And who better to bring him his supplies than whoever it was running that
show up there? So I come right out and asked him.

You know anything about mull? I said.

About where?

Pot, I said. Marijuana.

Oh, I see. No, I'm not your man for that.

Someone's growing it. Next door. Up there.

What?

Underground. They're growing skunk.

He looked at me like a total mong.

Weed, I said.

Drugs, you mean?

No, I said. They're running a fucking zoo. Of course it's
drugs, you dozy prick.

But Jaxie, how do you know this?

Because I stuck me head in, I said. Like a bloody stupid idiot.
I dug it up and looked in, that's how. They're running a genny
day and night to keep the lights on and the pumps going. It's
hydro. And not like a coupla kids growing up a few buds, it's
a professional outfit, someone heavy. A whole sea container,

maybe more than one, I didn't climb down to see how far it went. Jesus, there might be two or three rooms of it down there.

I see.

Yeah? Thing is, you don't look real surprised.

Surprised? Well, I am. Of course I'm surprised. But I just need a moment, now. Marijuana, you say?

They would of had machines in. Excavator, crane. You didn't hear nothing at all? Like a coupla semitrailers? Shit, Fintan, they've had a bulldozer going.

Well, I have the tinnitus, you see.

The what?

Tinnitus, he said. Of the ears. It's like a wretched wireless in your head.

You mean you hear voices?

Don't be soft, boy. Noises, it is, day and night.

Noises.

Good God, a torment of noise, boy. Like a radio signal that's never quite on the channel. Tinnitus!

Never heard of it, I said. Sounds like bullshit to me.

Well, lad, I'm half deaf, it's true, but it's not silence I have to contend with. Everything has to fight its way in through this infernal cacophony. Some days I have an hour or two of blessed relief. The rest of the time I wonder if anything at all I'm hearing is real. You understand me?

But you hear stuff. I know you do.

Yes, he said, some. But I lip-read, too. You must have noticed.

But when I first come here you twigged pretty quick. Don't lie, you heard me then.

No, he said. Not really. But I did feel you there. And I told you so. Even if I didn't quite believe in you, I felt you out there. Though in the end, of course, I saw you – remember? What is it, lad? What's put the fear in you?

This is fucking gangsters, I told him. Bad people. Right next door. And you want me to think you didn't know about it?

But lad, I hadn't the slightest notion.

How do I know you're not bullshitting me? You've got a shotgun. You could be working for them.

Drug dealers? Are you touched, boy? You think I'd stoop so low?

Drug dealing worse than kiddy fiddling, is it?

Stop that, now! There's no need and you've no right.

You think the Catholics care how they make their money? They bloody love gangsters, it's their bread and butter.

Good God, child, you wouldn't know the half of it. You wouldn't have the faintest notion.

I'm not a fucking child.

Well, you're talking like a fog-witted gombeen and it's no credit to you. And I see you didn't clean that rifle at all, he said. You'll be having misfires if you don't see to it.

Fuck you, I said. You're not the boss of me.

And then he laughed and threw his tin plate down and I really might of blown a hole in him big enough to walk through if the Browning hada been clean enough.

Oh, Jaxie, he said. I am in awe of you.

Stop saying that.

Rightso.

Fucksake.

Then it was quiet between us. Just the fire at our feet. And birds twitching in the trees as dark come down slowly. Fintan scratched his whiskery neck. I didn't know how to read him anymore. But it didn't seem smart to leave a caretaker like Fintan MacGillis out here. An old dude with no wheels. And so far away from what he was supposed to be watching.

So, he said. We have neighbours, you say.

Like I been telling you.

But you didn't see anyone?

There's no one there, I said. The setup runs itself. But it needs fuel and water so they'll have to be coming and going. They'll have to cut the stuff, plant more. Whatever the fuck they do.

Language, boy.

Oh piss off and get serious! It's not safe here.

But if it's all as you say, those lads have been going about their business up for there some time. Months, perhaps years, for all I know. And me none the wiser.

They're too close.

But they've not given us any bother. I'll wager they don't even know we're here. After all, we have no motors, rarely even fire a gun. If their little operation is as far up the lake as you say, perhaps there's not so much to worry about, even then. They're miles away.

I knew by then what Fintan was doing. He was trying to talk himself into feeling safe. It was him who was like a kid that way.

Anyroad, he said, have they not heard of the solar power, these lads?

What in the living fuck are you talking about?

Then they'd have no need to be running a generator and carting petrol.

Jesus, I said. You're an expert now? You haven't even got a panel yourself. You could be running a fridge out here.

Don't think I haven't mentioned that every Christmas and Easter, Jaxie boy. Any mission station south of the Sahara will have a bit of solar now. But it's not for the likes of Fintan MacGillis, you see. Wouldn't want to take the punitive edge off things, would they?

You're not right in the head, I said. Anyway these pricks wouldn't use solar panels.

And why not? Is it you the expert now?

Too easy to spot from the air. The cops are always looking for shit like that.

Really so? And how many aircraft have you seen since you've been out this way, lad?

I thought about it and shook me head.

There's no one looking, Jaxie. Not for them. Nor for you, I suspect. And I'd like to think not even for me.

I thought about that for a sec. And could be he was right. Could be I was panicking over nothing. They probably had no idea we was here.

But then I thought about them blokes growing mull. They were dead careful about keeping their deal secret. And this past few weeks I'd been out north shooting off and on. What's the odds they were never gunna hear the sound of a rifle in all that time? Or one of them would never get curious or bored enough to drive down the lake a little way? I sure wasn't gunna be there for that. It wouldn't really be any safer now back at the diggings. Too close to the highway if they were coming and going every week or two. No, it was clearer in me mind than ever, I was outta there. I'd creep on past that setup, keep heading north until I run out of lake altogether.

So I figured even while we were talking this would be my last night here at the shepherd's hut.

I was wrong of course. Though I was only out by a day or so. But I wish I'd pissed off right then. I shoulda shut Fintan's yap for him, yanked him off his arse and got us moving. That night. That very moment. Because now I know we coulda walked straight up the lake in the moonlight all night and been safe as money.

But that night by the fire with me guts full and me legs aching, all the hurry was leaked out of me. Now I'd said everything I had to say and got through to him there was no charge left. I was shagged and sore and I still hadn't cleaned the shit out of me rifle. And me duds were all strung out wet on the line, socks and all. Tomorrow would have to do. Give the old man time to pack some stuff. By noon we should both be set to go. A few hours wouldn't make much diff. That's what I told meself. Seems you're smarter looking back.

And here's the thing. Fintan musta known this spot wasn't safe anymore. He stopped arguing, just give up trying to convince himself. And though he never come out and said he was ready to go next morning I think he knew this was it. But he'd been out there a long time by then, the shepherd's hut was as close to a home as he was gunna get. So it wasn't easy for him to up stumps.

Would you take a turn with me, lad? he asked.

What?

Is it you hard of hearing now?

What is it? I said, pretty cranky. Can't you see I'm rooted?

Just a stroll on the lake, boy. To watch the moonrise.

With all this cloud? You're tapped.

Suit yourself, then.

He got up and dusted down his shorts like he was keeping himself nice and civilized but really he was buying time, guilting me. And I told meself no way. Fuck that. But in the end I got up bitching like a schoolkid and went along with him.

We carried our milk crates out through the samphire and it was hardly even dark when the first bump of moon peeped up across the lake. The whole of it come up quick, round and toasted like a Jatz cracker.

Behold, said Fintan.

Just the moon, I said. Same as last night.

No, no, tonight it's truly full.

Fine, I said. Not the same as last night. But it's still just the moon, isn't it.

Ah, he said. Look at that, will ye.

I am looking.

But don't you cower a little inside to see it? See how it drags itself up, bigger, stranger, more powerful by the minute. Like something hatching and growing before your eyes. Doesn't some small part of you shrivel in awe?

No, I said, which wasn't exactly the truth.

Not even a moment of creaturely wonder?

Then I told him Auntie Marg wouldn't let us sleep outside on a full moon. She said we'd get moon lunacy.

Moon lunacy, indeed!

The bullshit they tell you, eh.

But you believed her, I think.

Fuck, I was six years old. She was me auntie.

You probably didn't need any convincing from her. But there it is, Jaxie lad, bigger than television. It's awesome – even a little intimidating, don't you think?

I dunno, I said. Maybe.

Son, I used to scoff at all the notions people got about the sun and moon. Primitive people, I mean. With all their worshipping and fearing. But the longer I'm out here. Well, it knocks the scoffing out of a fella.

While he nattered on I watched the moon crank itself up higher. With all them clouds stewing and streaking round it that thing did look kind of badarse.

When I was a lad, said Fintan, five years old, mebbe six, I thought the moon was watching me. I'd come out into the yard of a summer's evening, off to the shed with the barrow for my mother, out to the turf pile for the fire. Some nights I could see my shadow trailing and the great white eye of it peering down. I tell you, I felt . . . transparent.

Like clean?

No, no. See-through. As if God, or the universe if you will, could read me like an open book.

I thought you weren't sure about God.

And I've no doubt he's had his second thoughts over the likes of me.

You think he knows you're bonkers?

I wonder.

And then I felt like a bit of a turd because Fintan went on and started talking about this for serious.

I know I'm not always in my right mind out here, Jaxie, I'll admit that much. Not my best mind, any rate. And not my old mind, either, but I don't regret that so much. Maybe you think it's the loneliness does it. Rightso, perhaps it is. But I suspect it's the place, now. Look at that, he said, waving at the milky shine of the lake, what a marvel! Night and day it's a wonder. You know, there are afternoons when I look down there to the south and see those stones walking in the sunlight.

Oh man, you and them rocks.

Yes, lad, I know. But listen, when they go all loose and watery in the heat, you'd swear they're dancing.

Yeah, whatever.

No, truly. It's as if they're limbering up, like warriors preparing for battle. You've seen them yourself all bunched up like a phalanx out there, bristling, pulsating. Some fearful, pagan part of a fella expects them to charge on down the lake.

Like, at you?

Exactly.

And what d'you think they're gunna do, ask for a cup of sugar?

Well, I don't really know. That's the thing of it. In the

moment it gets me very apprehensive. But excited, all the same. Sometimes I get this quare feeling they've come for me, to hold me to account.

What, interrogate you sorta thing?

Something like that. Yes. Oh indeed. I have dreams about it. Often, now. And in these dreams they move like people. They come in off the salt, silent as ghosts, and they stand in by the fire. But they never say a thing.

Well they're fricken rocks, I said.

Perhaps.

Then what do they do?

They just watch, boy. And listen.

That's fucked up.

Disconcerting, yes.

How many are there? These walking rocks.

Oh, five or six that come in close. Maybe a hundred stand off back towards the lake. And I can feel them taking me in, sizing me up. And in the dream, every time, I'm certain they know all my darkest secrets. They see right into me, Jaxie. And I'm frightened and ashamed and I want to tell them everything.

Like confess?

Aye.

All your sins and whatnot?

All of it.

But they're rocks!

You see, that's the thing. In the dream they never seem so rock-like. They're bigger, of course, the size of you and me. And there's a grandness to them, something severe and monumental.

It makes the heart race, lad. And I am afraid each time they appear, very fearful, but then I feel their great dispassion, their purity. I can trust them with everything I know, everything I fear. And the relief of knowing that, Jaxie. I can't begin to tell you.

That's whack.

Indeed.

So you tell them stuff? These bloody rocks.

Yes, said Fintan. That is, I begin to. I take a breath to spill it all. And then I wake. Like a man fallen short once more. And it's crushing. Terrible.

Geez.

Terrible, he says again, like he's there still trapped in the nightmare.

Well, I said, to buck him up, it's just a dream.

Ah, perhaps it is. And nothing more. Who knows, Jaxie? Maybe it's the stones and trees who'll be our judges in the end.

And the goats and roos?

Could be so.

And the birds?

Oh, especially the birds.

I laughed and he laughed a bit and ducked his head and scuffed his boots in the samphire.

You're one druggy fucker.

Oh lad, I know they're only stones. And the moon is only the moon. But they're not empty things, you know. The past is still in them. The force of events long gone, it lingers. These heavenly bodies and earthly forms, what are they but expressions

TIM WINTON

of matters unfinished? Perhaps it's not childish nonsense to see stones as men walking, to behold the moon and feel a tinge of dread. A stone is a fact, a consequence. And the moon, it marks a man's days, does it not? Another month gone, a reminder every cycle that your moment is waning. No wonder it catches in a little fella's chest when he sees it. Mebbe lunatics are men who've remembered they're just men, not angels.

Jesus, I said. That's what you come out to see the moon for, to remember you're gunna die?

No, he said. To remember I am a creature, not a ghost. I am, for all my sins, the thing itself, not just the idea. Ah, look at that moon. Still rising, rising. Like the wafer. Forever out of reach. When I close my eyes it burns in my head. And Jaxie, how I wish that afterglow would light my way. To sleep. To peace.

So, I said after a bit. Who does a priest confess to?

Whatsay?

You priests, I said. Who do you tell your shit to? Another priest?

He shrugged, like that was his half-arsed yes.

And it's secret forever?

Fintan turned his hands over, feeling his knuckles. He was clear in the moonlight. His mouth was all puckered.

But you'd rather go to a stone instead. Tell that all your secrets.

Aye, I would.

Because that's all you can trust?

I'm not sound, Jaxie. I'm not proud of it.

228

They've kicked you out, haven't they?

No, he said. That might have been a mercy. But I'm still a priest.

You don't even believe in it.

The priesthood? I don't know.

God, I mean.

He shrugged again.

That's a bit piss-weak, I said.

Indeed, I suppose it is.

So how long were you in the job?

Oh, he said. Well, let's see. I was a lad. And then I was a priest. So, what's that, then, fifty years, give or take?

And you didn't believe in God?

Jaxie, you're not a believer yourself – how can any of this matter to the likes of you?

Well, I'm not a fucking priest, am I? How can you be a priest and not believe in God?

I don't know, he said. Sometimes you do. The rest of the time you settle for just believing in the Church. It's like family, lad. What else do we have?

Don't ask me, I said. I haven't got a family.

Well, that's a pair of us here, wouldn't you say?

The moon was higher now and shrinking. The colour was leaking out of it. Soon the lake and the moon were pale as each other, like the inside of Lee's leg, creamy enough to make you hurt just looking.

Aw cut the shit, I said, boiling over all of a sudden. What the fuck did you do, Fintan?

It doesn't matter what I did.

Geez, it must of mattered to someone if it's got you in this much trouble.

That's not what I meant. Of course it mattered. It affected a lot of people. The consequences were monstrous, unthinkable, unspeakable, unforgiveable. But I won't be confessing any of it to you.

You don't trust me.

Wrong. Untrue.

You'd only trust a rock.

Hell's teeth, boy, don't you think you've seen and suffered enough? Do you think for my own ease I'd pour all that on you, too?

I don't care. I can take it.

You shouldn't have to take it, and you don't know enough to care. I mean that kindly, now.

Well fuck.

I know.

I just couldn't stand it if you were a pedo.

Dear God, he said. If I were one of those do you think I'd be out here in Gehenna? I'd be off in some rainswept parish. I'd be riding the Salthill bus. I'd be tucked up in bed by the bay in Galway.

I don't get you people.

So you keep saying, boy. But it's like this. And I'll try to keep it simple, because for a man like me, under the great mercy of order and discipline as I've been, life should be simple. There're only three things can get a priest into serious trouble. That's doctrine, sex and money. In the case of the first two, discretion will generally keep a fella safe. I shut up, they shut up, and all will be well. But where money is concerned, no secret will hold.

It took a sec for any of that to make sense. But it hit me like a slap.

Are you shitting me? I said. This is just about money?

The want of it, the power of it. The excitement in it. The consequences of it. These are not small things, lad.

Jesus fuck.

When you're older you'll see this for yourself, sad to say.

I got up then. I couldn't stand any more.

You're pathetic, I said. All of you.

He didn't say nothing to that. I didn't even look at him. I took me crate and left him there.

Up at the hut I lit the hurricane lamp and fluffed the fire up and put the billy on for a brew before bed. I dunno why I was so bummed. I should of been glad he wasn't a rock spider. But whatever he was he wouldn't say. And maybe that was it. Knowing he was never going to. He would always have this secret thing. And I felt like such a tool. It was a mistake to think we were on the square, like equals, because it wasn't like that, never would be. But then I thought of Lee and all the things about her, stuff right deep in me I didn't want to share with anybody, him included. Half of it he wouldn't get anyway, he just wasn't ready for that sort of information. He'd look at me like I was a filthy savage. But he couldn't help that, he was just another flaky fuckup pretending to be full grown. And thinking of it that way some of the sting went out of me. I was sad but not so mad. I sat and looked round, kind of taking everything in one last time, and the billy hissed and mumbled and finally it come to the boil.

I made a brew and when it was ready I poured a pannikin for meself and one for Fintan. But he didn't come up and I figured he wanted to sulk and watch the moon without the likes of me. His tea was cold and mine was drunk when he shuffled in and dropped his crate by the fire.

I'm just heading off, I said.

But where, lad?

Bed, I told him.

Oh. Yes.

I'm cactus.

Cactus, he said. Yes, indeed. You're that, I'll grant you.

Right, I said getting up.

Before you go, now, I wanted to clear something up. Although I doubt it'll be of use to either of us, and probably clarify nothing at all.

It doesn't matter, I said.

Well, it does. Because I don't want to give you wrong ideas. I don't want to add to your confusion if I can help it. And I'm hardly a man to turn to for wisdom, but you deserve an honest answer to something.

Look, I said. It's no odds to me.

Mebbe so. You say that now, but you asked me what I believe, Jaxie. About God.

That's none of my business, I said. Tell it to the rocks.

But I can't. This is the point, lad. This is the rusty hook I dangle from. In some pain, I'm not too proud to add. Perhaps I'll never settle it, never be coherent, let alone sound. But I suspect that God is what you do, not what or who you believe in.

Well. Whatever.

You understand me? It's what you do.

But people do shit things all the time, I said. There's something wrong with us.

Perhaps. And maybe not. But when you do right, Jaxie, when you make good – well, then you are an instrument of God. Then you are joined to the divine, to the life force, to life itself. That's what I believe. That's what I hope for. And it's what I have missed.

That's all jumblyfuck to me, I said as decent as I could.

Well, think of it this way, he said, pushing his specs back up his nose. When somebody does me a kindness, it enlarges me, adds to my life, you see? And not only mine – it adds to all life. Which is why I wanted to thank you. For coming here.

Me?

Fintan give a sad little laugh. And I caught him looking at me goony as an emu.

What? I said.

Don't you understand me, boy? Can't you see it? Jaxie Clackton, you are an instrument of God.

Oh, I said. You mad fucker. You been out under the moon too long!

And we both of us laughed.

I am in earnest, boy.

Get fucked, I said still laughing.

Think on it.

And I left him there with that look on his face and the flamelight running up his legs.

Back at me swag at last I layed down and pulled the sheet up and thought about him a while. All his ten-dollar words and priesty shit. Instrument of God. It was priceless, a bloke carrying on like that. It was like he had too many words in him to just come out and say we was square and equal. Sometimes it was like Fintan was drowning in his own talk. And I wondered what that might be like. Us Clacktons never done our thinking out aloud. Or our talking neither really. Wankbag only ever talked about what he could hold in his hand. Before he closed his fist on it and clubbed you with it. And Mum, I wonder if she ever could tell me what she wanted. In the end she had nothing to say to me at all. Maybe too much talk's better than that.

And it's curious how Fintan could be so old and lost and sorry and fucked up and still see so clear and far. He got me somehow, that's one thing for certain. Makes sense in a way because we put in bulk time together, those months there was no one else to turn to. But it was strange how he got Lee as well, when I never let on, never said. Still, he knew what she was like. Not just her eyes and shaved head and whatnot, that's the outside. It was like he knew how solid she is, and brave, how she adds to life, the way he said, how she makes the world bigger just by being in it.

Look, I always knew he was a bullshit artist. Thing is, most of that was outside too, like camo sorta thing. But there was some hot feeling he give off once you knew him. It was like you were standing too close to the stove or coming over with a fever. And I only ever had it with one other person before and that was Lee. It's a dangerous feeling getting noticed, being wanted. Getting seen deep and proper, it's shit hot but terrible too. It's like being took over. And your whole skin hurts like you suddenly grew two sizes in a minute.

That last night there's words I would of said to Fintan if I hadna been so rooted, if I'd of known what tomorrow'd bring down on us. Things I should of got up off me swag to tell him. Not about me really, not even about Lee or Monkton or Magnet. Just things about him I should of thought to say. I guess he done some horrible things and I reckon he was a pretty bunky priest but I knew he was more than any of that.

And I wish I could say I stayed up late thinking about him but the truth is I was only awake a little while. I was so tired the swag felt like a sponge that soaked me up. I went to sleep like someone disappearing from the earth, like rain sopped into dust.

I woke up in the night to another noise. A kind of clunk. Like somebody was there. I sat up real slow and remembered I'd left the Browning in the hut. I didn't even have a knife with me. The pack was still out there under the verandah.

The moon was gone behind me now but it still lit everything plain enough. The hut was quiet, no one to see anywhere near it. The lake was so bright it looked like a sea of milk. And the windmill was clear against it and its blades weren't turning. I took a few secs to cop the white flash underneath it. Rising and falling. It was just a goat trying to figure its way out of the yard. It jumped against the gate and hacked along the fence. It was nothing.

I slid back under me sheet and pulled the canvas flap up a little way because the air was chilling off a bit. The goat kept at it down there, clacking and pigrooting. A coupla times it give out a bleat but it didn't keep me awake long.

But I dreamt I come home here again. Walked in by the killing tree. Back from a long trek sore and hungry. And there was a goat hung up on the gambrel. And me mouth run with spit. I walked faster, to see how far the old man had got with it, wondered how long it might be till we got some meat on the grill. But when I come by close I saw it wasn't even skun yet. And it was too big for a goat. Too thick for a roo even. There was blood strung out black from its toes and I saw they were me own feet there lifted off the dirt, me bare legs all bruised and dirty, me dick shrivelled small as a snail, and I looked up into that face and saw I was a beast with all the wildness bled out of him.

I don't spose I'll ever know if things coulda worked out different. But I been thinking about it, wondering if it was all my fault. Asking meself if everything mighta gone better if only I stayed keyed up that night and hadna gone off the boil.

I know I shoulda kept savage. Right from when I come back to the hut. Shoulda told Fintan to shut his cakehole the second he started up with his clean-freak carry-on. Just layed down the law then and there, even if I had to shove a gun in his face again for his own sake. Because when I staggered back in from the north I already knew it was war we had. If we didn't piss off straight away some serious shit would go down. And if anything needed cleaning first up it was the fucking rifle, not me. But by then I was so used to his gobbing and nagging. Used to giving in just to keep the peace. Now I can see there was no time to explain right then, no time to argue about what to make of all this news, no time to rest up and start fresh in the morning. It was then we shoulda gone.

Taking that bath was the first mistake. It took the edge off. Slowed me down. When I shoulda been getting sorted straight away, shoving Fintan inside, filling a pack for him and handing him his shotgun and shells I was letting the old bugger talk, leaving him to make everything feel normal. Because that was him. He could throw enough words at something to smother it. Like you toss a blanket on a fire. Oh if only I got him up and going. Then he could of crapped on all night, talking on the march. That was the thing but. He could talk the hardness out of you. What happened was I give in to being hungry, give in to feeling zombie tired. And if I'da stayed hard and kept smart I woulda got straight down to business, I know it. Seen to me kit. The waterjug. Backpack. The Browning. I woulda seen what was missing.

And yeah, then everything *would* of been different. All of it. We coulda hiked out north, fixed me horrible mistake and kept on up the lake. And give ourselves five more hours, maybe even twelve. Them hours, they woulda made all the difference. True, I wouldn't be on the road today if things had gone down otherwise. But I wouldna spent yesterday burying people neither.

Still you can't keep doing the coulda and the woulda and the shoulda. This isn't about what didn't happen. And if there's one thing I know it's this. Doesn't matter how smart you are, or even how careful or lucky, there's some mistakes you just keep

making over and over. And they're the ones that fuck you up
and get people hurt.

What did happen is I slept past dawn, way past. In the end
Fintan had to come up and wake me, I was that sore and fucked
up. He cooked us a feed of chops and fried a coupla munted
tomatoes and made a brew strong enough to leave rust in your
veins. And we was both quiet, a bit embarrassed after last night
maybe and I was trying to make a plan while we got the feed
in. Fintan did that old man thing he did, like he was chewing
doublegees with them plastic teeth of his. I tried to ignore it.
I was pissed off at meself. I knew I'd have to push like hell
to get him ready to go now. It shoulda been me waking him
before first light, getting him cracking. But I could see he was
already faffing over what books to take, still thinking it hadn't
come down to the four things you can carry. On your back, in
your hand, over your shoulder, round your neck.

And that's when I thought of it. When I got up to check.

The pack was still under the verandah. The dirty .243 next to
it. The waterjug empty on its side right behind them.

I went in the hut and looked round but I already knew they
wouldn't be there. Them fucking binoculars. I knew exactly
where they were.

I didn't even stop long enough to get dressed properly. All
me camo clobber was still wet and strung out on the wire so
I went out in them baggy shorts and that polo shirt of his.
I pulled me boots on barefoot and laced them extra tight. I told
him to take water and ammo and hide up the ridge and wait
till I come back. And if I didn't he should wait till the moon

come up and get out on the lake and walk till he come to the salt mine. There'd be water there. If it turned out I didn't make it that far there might be people decent enough to take him in.

But he wasn't listening. I knew it then. He thought I was bullshitting him, that this was just my way of pissing off and leaving him there on his own. And if he hadn't of been tugging at me and following me to the tank again I might of remembered me hat at least, and taken some food. But it was a fucking scene, a full on circus. He begged me not to go. Actually got on his knees. And I was that disgusted, that bloody panicked I nearly give him one. It was all I could do to pull him off and yank meself away.

He called after me. You, he said. Jaxie. You're the one, boy. It was always you. You're the man.

And I thought, yeah. I'm the one got us in the shit, it's me who put us in danger, and maybe the old nutbag's right, maybe I am the end of days.

I hoisted the rifle and jug and got running. And right from the start that pack pounded at me, punching me low in the back like it wasn't ever gunna let me forget.

No word of a lie, that last day was a hell march. Backing up and doing that trip again, it was harsh. Fucking near killed me. Though least this time I knew where I was going. Which shoulda made it faster. But I was tight and sore from the get-go and panicky too, which didn't help. Yesterday I was only curious and worried, now I didn't know if I was too scared or not nearly scared enough. Those jokers up there might not be back for weeks. But the way that genny was sounding yesterday I figured it'd be sooner rather than later. Could be they were there already. Looked like they'd been at this game a while, they'd know how long a tank of petrol lasted. I tried not to think about that. Just cracked on running all the way. And pretty soon I was blowing raw.

About halfway I rested a minute under a piddly little sheoak.
I had a sip and looked at all the shit caked in the barrel of
the .243. Figured it wasn't gunna be much use like that. So I
pulled out the Dexter and cut a long piece off of Fintan's shorts.
But then I realized I had nothing to use as a rod. No gun oil
neither. Not even any goat fat. I'd have to wait till I found
a decent twitch of fencewire or a piece of steel, even better.
And then scour the barrel out dry, which couldn't be good.
Or maybe I could gob in it for lubrication. Anything was better than having it plugged up with red grit. I thought of that
wrecked F-truck up ahead. There'd be something on that for
sure. A steel rod. Engine oil. Even steering fluid. So I stuffed
the strip of rag in me pocket, pulled meself into shape and got
going again.

I never run so hard and so far in all me life. At school they
couldn't even get me to jog round the oval. But there's this thing
that happens once you been going long enough, this feeling you
can go forever. Maybe I was a bit tapped by then but I got this
idea I was made to do this. I was hard and lean and gnarly. And
now I'd run the panic out I was fuck-off determined too. All I
needed was speed. And some luck. And if I didn't get lucky I'd
want a clean gun. So for a long while I didn't think about those
jokers up there. They were strangers I might not even meet.
What I stuck to was getting the Browning sorted. That meant
making it to the effy. Everything else was too far in the future.

I don't know how long it took to get up into the neighbours'
place. But when I found the old fencewire in the weeds at the
boundary corner I had no cutters or even pliers. And that F100

was no use at all. It was full of dry buffel grass and snaky as shit. I got clutch fluid all over me hands and tried for a while to get a gas strut off the back of the thing but me fingers were greasy and it was hopeless without tools anyway. After a few minutes wasted on that caper I had to settle for pulling the bolt out of the rifle and blowing down the bore. Which did five-eighths of fuck all. Then I rubbed me hands through the dirt, took another sip from the Igloo and went on.

I spose it was near on lunchtime when I got up the last ridge and scooched in on me belly to scan the valley with the rifle scope.

There wasn't a soul about that I could see. Only one thing was different to yesterday. No generator noise. Out of juice.

And it wasn't like I needed any motivating but that didn't half give me the hurry-up.

I got to me feet and got running. Only had them stupid binoculars to get and I'd be outta there. I was more than half-way down to the clearing before I copped the shine off the windscreen. Up along the spine of the ridge in the west. Just a half a second of flash and I hit the dirt like I'd been shot, went face down in a dive that knocked the wind out of me. And it took a dog's age before I even heard that vehicle come janking slow and steady down the track. Stones pinging, suspension squeaking. All I had for cover was knee-high saltbush. So I kept flat and still. Didn't dare look up. Not when it rumbled to a stop. Not even when the engine give out.

For a little while the only sound was crows. I had the urge to feel round for me waterjug and rifle and pull them in tight so they couldn't give me away but I had the pack still strapped on, that bright blue piece of shit, and it was stuck up there like a turtle shell on the back of me. Soon as I moved to pull it off they'd see me bright and clear. So I just made meself flat and swivelled bit by bit, real careful, to get a glimpse. I looked slantways at them like they were roos I was hunting. Man, I was peering through me fucking eyebrows in the end.

The car was one of them tinny Jeep things. Cherokee. Station wagon. With shiny polished mags. And a petrol engine. A real townie car. It had a horse float hooked on behind that looked big as a caravan. I saw two blokes, one with a dinky straw hat and one with long dark hair. The dude with the hat was the driver. He got out, stepped my way a little and took a piss. The other one went round to the trailer and unlatched the back. The first dude shook himself off, give a shiver and then helped his mate drop the ramp. The driver went up into the float. He passed something out. A red plastic jerry can. The longhaired one took it and stood it on the dirt and soon another one was handed out, then more. They worked like that till there was maybe ten of those things lined up next to the trailer, 25-litre jerries, all full by the looks.

Then the driver passed down a long-handled shovel. And I always knew this was gunna happen, there was no other way it could go, I'd played it all in me head already but when I saw that thing come out I nearly let off a groan. All I could do was hope I was wrong. But I knew I wasn't wrong. The longhair swung the shovel to his shoulder and stepped out to the soft dug dirt where everything was buried. By then I couldn't help but lift me head for a better view and fuck me if there wasn't a wodge of prints round the edge even I could see from this far out. But I don't think he noticed them because when he called out he was right over where the hatch should be, there on the dirt I'd swept down so careful with a sheoak branch. And I knew what he was gunna see before he stopped and looked down. But I still twitched when I heard him.

Fuck! was all he said.

And there they were, swinging in his hand, those bloody glasses.

The driver was halfway past the car by then. He had a steel crate like an ammo box in his arms and when he heard his mate yell he dropped it flat. From the sound it made I figured it was full of tools, not bullets. He half ran out to where the dude was pigrooting round with his Adidas and getting all excited. Straight away they both started scoping every which way. I just shoved me face into the pebbles and tried to make meself invisible.

Pretty soon I heard the shovel and the trapdoor. I snuck a peek and saw one guy kneeling and talking to the other one down the ladder. He passed down a torch. Right then I knew my best chance to bolt was when the second bloke got himself down the hatch too. I might be gone before they saw me and even if they copped a glimpse I'd have a head start. But the driver bastard never climbed in.

I wasn't even fifty metres out. The ground sloped up behind so me boots were higher than me head. Between where I was and the rim of the ridge back there it was more or less open ground, just saltbush. And that was no small stretch of country to get up and across. They'd see me in a heartbeat. And even if they didn't have anything to shoot me with, even if I got up there and into the mulga before they could get their shit together and chase me down with the car, I'd have given meself away. And Fintan too. Unless they were real city fuckwits, all they'd have to do was find me with those glasses or follow me tracks.

But if I stayed put and waited till they left, maybe I had half a chance of getting home to warn Fintan. Could be now they had the wind up they'd camp here for the night to keep an eye out. That was gunna be tough for me but better than no chance at all. I figured in the dark I'd have pretty decent odds of getting away clean.

But fuck me, they were taking a year to make their minds up. The longhair was underground for ages. When he climbed out he chucked something on the dirt, the torch I think, and then the two of them were flapping their hands and arguing, quiet as they could, till in the end they calmed down a bit. Then they dropped the hatch and shovelled dirt back and smoothed the ground real quick, rough as bags. Longhair went to the trailer and started hoiking jerries in. The driver in the hat snatched up the glasses and hung them round his neck. He shoved the torch in his pocket and walked out to the mulga edge, broke a bit off a little jam and used it to sweep everything clear of prints. The numbnuts, he even wiped out mine. Then he went back to the Jeep. Ditched the torch and binocs in the window and took the heavy box to the ramp.

After that they were a while getting the rest of the petrol in the horse float. I couldn't make out anything they said but you could tell it was snarly. In the end they hoisted the ramp and latched it and went to the vehicle. Longhair opened his door and reached in and pulled out a pistol. An automatic. I saw it across the bonnet. He drew the slide and I heard it snap back from where I was. Then both of them got in and the engine cranked over and they spent five minutes jinning about, trying to back the float up to turn round the way they come. City fellas, no question. Them muppets couldn't reverse a trailer for shit. In the end they had the thing totally jackknifed and any other time it woulda been bloody hilarious. Anyway after a bit more pissing about and heaps of shouting they got out and unhitched the thing, left it on the jockey wheel and took off without it. They were fully peaking, these dudes. I felt better about them all the time.

But they weren't gone yet. Hardly a hundred metres up the track they jammed on the anchors, pulled up in a cloud of dust and had themselves a right old blue. Screaming, finger pointing, arsing and cunting, full catastrophe. Longhair slapped the side of the car through his open window so hard I jumped. Against that tinny piece-of-shit Jeep it sounded like a .410 going off. And I thought Jesus, any moment one of these jokers is gunna blow the other one's brains out. They're mental.

Come on you cockheads, I said to meself. Make your minds

up. Get on with it. Go! And for fucksake don't turn back this way, head for the highway, don't go down the lake track. And that's a joke on me, I know, praying to utter bastards.

But in the end they didn't go down the lake track. Probably didn't even know about it. And it was pretty faint and grown over, true. They rumbled on up along the ridge and where the fork come they followed the track west. I just hoped and wished they were scuttling back to the city but I knew if that was what they were planning they wouldna left the horse float. West, though, that was towards the highway.

I can't say I wasn't curious about what else was in that big trailer. I saw all I needed to see later. But there wasn't time for that now.

The moment they got over the crest and out of sight I was up and running again.

I went that hard on the trip back, way faster than on the way out. Because I knew we were truly in the shit now, me and Fintan. But most of that afternoon it felt like I was running on the spot. I had too much time to wonder where them city boys were, what they were planning to do, how far they'd got. If I was them I'd of put the time in looking for tracks, worked me way out from the dope in circles. Get a direction first. I knew from hunting food the thing you need most of isn't water or ammo, it's patience. But these characters, they couldn't imagine any-one hoofing it out here. Already had it in their heads I was in a car. So they'd follow every two-rut they come across. But there could be dozens of them. Who knew how many tracks were out here across this stretch of prospecting country? If they were halfway smart they'd see pretty quick it was a waste of time chasing down every old car track they come to. They'd go out the way they come. If they saw nothing by the time they got to the highway they'd drive up and down it looking for other ways in. Whoever got in here had to come off the main road. They had to be able to nut that much out. And if they did and drove south a few minutes they'd soon see a slip-off running east. The miners' track, the one to the diggings and the prospector's shack. They'd be there quick enough. They'd see the roo I left hanging out the front. After all this time it might be nothing but bones but they'd see plain as dick that someone'd been there and if they checked the shack they'd find whatever shit I left behind. They'd push on down to the lake. By then they'd know for sure that people were about. They'd be toey as all hell. And once they got down to the shore they could drive flat out down the lake, following me footprints. And Fintan wouldn't even hear them coming.

If they knew what they were doing all this might take only a coupla hours, tops. But they might get lucky and do it quicker. So I was hoping they navigated about as good as they backed a trailer. And it wouldn't hurt if they were a little bit unlucky as well. The tracks out there were rough as guts. I needed them to take a few wrong turns, maybe stake a tyre. Even better if they busted an axle. Otherwise I had the awful feeling they were gunna beat me home.

It's one thing to think someone's stupid. And fair enough if you need them to be. But you can't go banking on it. That's a mug's game.

So I pounded back through the mulga. Nearly ditched the waterjug because it slowed me down so much but in the end I hooked the handle over the rifle barrel and let it thump me shoulder every step I took. It was deadset irritating but it was like some little piggybacking bastard kicking me on, it kept me hard at it.

Somewhere down the lake I started wondering if I wasn't twisting off about nothing. Who's to say these jokers were even serious about looking for us? After all there was nothing of theirs missing back there. I didn't touch a thing down that ladder, never even got in to take a proper look. What was the use in hitting the panic button? And if they thought it was the cops and there was some big sting going down, wouldn't they just fuck off and stay away forever? Me, I'd torch everything, the whole bunker, leave no evidence. But they'd left the horse float, hadn't they? And it'd be full of incriminating evidence, DNA and whatnot.

But the cops don't leave binoculars laying round. That's only what a normal idiot does. So they'd figure it wasn't cops, they had to know it was the genny give them away. And who else'd hear that but people living close by or someone camping along the lake? They were like us, these dudes, they'd never even dreamt there was anyone else out here. Not until them glasses. No, they wouldn't just be curious. They were jumpy as fuck. Saw that with me own eyes. That and the pistol. I knew I was right to be worried. These cunts would be trouble.

When I got to the lake I had a blow and took a swallow and thought real hard about heading straight out onto the saltpan and bolting home that way. No question it'd be quicker. But then I'd be out in the open. Even if I hadn't seen a gun already I wouldna given up the cover to make time. That just wasn't smart. So I kept back in from the shore, running the rocky edges through the saltbush and mulga.

And I'd be one lying bastard if I said I never thought about pissing off and getting away clean. Fact is I didn't have to keep on south like that. Except for me duds I didn't have to go back to the shepherd's hut at all. I could of cut back north. Hugged the shore till I found the saltworks. Or gone deep into the canyon country where there was no vehicle tracks at all. Those numbnuts wouldn't come in after me on foot. Fintan MacGillis, that old motormouth, he was no family to me.

So yeah, I thought about it alright. For a while it was all I could think about. But I kept on south anyway. Because I knew whatever was gunna happen was my fault. It was me responsible.

I don't know how far I got before I put me foot down the goanna hole. One moment I'm plugging along with all this crap going through me head. Next thing I'm face down in the gravel between the jam bushes and me knee's so bad I don't even feel the stake through me hand till I'm squeezing me leg like I'm trying to strangle the pain out of it, and I cop this thin hard spear of mulga wood, long as a finger, going right through the meat of me thumb. The point of it stuck up clean and grey and for a sec there wasn't even any blood. The knee hurt a lot worse but the look of that thing coming through me hand made me bum quiver. When I yanked it out it bled like I'd struck oil. Jesus, what a mess. I had to sit there for a bit, get me shit together.

For a while I couldn't even get up, let alone walk. And there was bull ants crawling over me like I was dead already and I figured it was better to get to me feet than be eaten alive, so I dragged meself up and hung off a jam wattle till I could man up and get going again.

So I did that. I drank off me water and ditched the jug. Got moving. But not real quick. And it wasn't long before I knew things weren't gunna go our way.

I don't even know how long it took me to get there. All I know is it was too long.

I saw the shine off the Jeep before I even copped the hut roof. It was parked along the lakeshore maybe half a click south. They come in just the way I dreaded. When I got in closer, trying to stay as low as the knee would let me, there was no sign of them or of the old man. And I knew odds were he hadn't listened to me. He wouldn't be hid up behind the ridge, the silly bugger. If he hadna seen them coming he'd be well in the shit already. I shrugged off the pack and used the .243 as a prop as I got belly down on the dirt. The knee hurt like a motherfucker.

I wondered how long I should wait. Then I heard his voice. That crazy bloody laugh. They were all inside the hut together.

Fintan was a sneaky old prick, he was twice as smart as he looked and about half as clever as he thought he was. But if he was still laughing things hadn't got nasty yet. I had time to do something to keep him safe. Thing was, I couldn't figure what that thing might be. I could shoot their windscreen out, give him a chance to run, but Fintan wasn't any sort of runner. And maybe before I did anything at all I needed to know what was happening. I had to get close. So I crawled in slow and bitsy like a half squashed bug. I hauled meself along with the Browning. And it took a while, but in the end I washed up in pretty much the same spot where I hid that first day. Same pebbly dirt, same thornybushes.

From there I could see the open door, the shutter poled out, no smoke from the chimney. And there were voices. Fintan's was easy to pick. You'd never miss that dancing Irish sound. The others were hard and blunt. But I couldn't see much, not even through the scope. The angle was bad and it was dim in there anyway and the light outside was hot and white.

Out front the billy was steaming in the coals. He was making them tea, the wily coot, giving them the priesty runaround, seeing if he couldn't still talk his way out of a corner. And this was one time I hoped he'd never shut up. Both of us needed all the time he could give us.

That was when I noticed the goat strung up on the gambrel. It was between me and the hut, right there in me face. Dunno how I didn't see it before. And honest, I could of spat. Because instead of hiding like I told him and waiting for me signal, the dozy old prick had gone down the mill yard and made himself busy. But he'd only got the beast half skun before those two jokers showed up. The goat looked like some unlucky schoolkid with his jumper pulled over his head.

Then Fintan give a yelp. Or it might of just been that laugh of his. Whatever it was I was twitchy as fuck now. I didn't like the look of any of this.

I wondered what me chances were of creeping up to the door. Surprise the shit out of them if I could get that far. But if both those pricks had guns and there's three people there in the dark and me suddenly lit up in the sunny doorway, well none of that was gunna go smooth and not much of it would go our way neither. But it still looked like the only chance I had. I thought about letting off a shithawk call to warn the old man I was on me way in, but tell the truth I couldn't work up the breath for it, I was panting like a mutt, sucking up the balls to make me move. And I was half a second from pushing up to go when the dude in the tiny hat showed in the doorway.

I caught him clear in the scope and saw he was a big shiny-skinned fella with earrings and a chipped tooth. He looks left and right and then behind him comes Fintan and the longhair after that, pulling down his mirror shades. The old priest's bare-chested and his shorts are halfway off his arse and there's blood all down his arms and belly, and for a sec I think they've been at him already but then I remember the goat.

I thought about the birdcall again. And then I said to meself what kind of stupid idea is this, giving a deaf bloke a noise for a signal? So I didn't make a sound. The scope got fuzzy and that was when I knew how bad I was shaking.

All three of them stood out in the yard a bit. And right in front of them the billy come to the boil, the lid started jumping and a tail of steam got up. Them blokes stood looking at it a sec. Fintan said loud and plain he best go in and get the makings for a brew, said it cheery as you like but if I could see the lumps in the back of them two's shirts from here he must of twigged they had guns by now. But there he was, nattering away like butter wouldn't melt in his mouth, edging his way back a little and I'm urging him on, go mate, get inside, grab the bloody shotgun.

I jacked a round into the chamber then and it sounded so loud and gritty I couldn't believe no one heard. I sighted on Fintan first. He was all smiles and twinkles but I could read him like a book. If he come out shooting I had to make sure I didn't hit him. The longhair was closer to the door, the blast from the shotty would knock him down. But the driver in the hat was further my way, it was him I had to hit. So I watched Fintan with one bare eye and sighted on the hat with the other.

But the driver's casing the yard. The windmill. The half skun goat.

No hurry, he says to Fintan. Don't go to any trouble.

Oh, no trouble, says Fintan, slopping back a way in his gumboots.

And then quick as a snake longhair is between him and the door and the old man's got that rolled-gold look of surprise on and I'm thinking ah, that's fucked it. The hat jerks his head at the goat on the gambrel.

Looks like we interrupted something, he goes.

No matter, says Fintan. She'll keep awhile. Long enough for a spot of tea. I can make a damper, if you fancy.

Maybe later, says the longhair behind his sunnies.

So, goes the hat, all curious and friendly, how long you been out here?

Whatsay?

Here. On this land. How long?

Fintan goes, Oh, a nun's age, now. I'm not the lessee, mind, I'm only a guest these days.

Okay, says the driver in the hat. Like a caretaker then?

Fintan just smiles.

So who owns the place? goes the hat.

Oh, some corporate shenanigan.

Foreigners, says the longhair. Chinese, I'll bet.

Well, goes Fintan. It's the way of it, these days.

Yep, says the hat. The poor old Australian farmer's becoming a thing of the past.

You're a man of the land yourself, then? asks Fintan.

Yeah, says the hat. More or less. We're looking at some property round this way.

Ah, says Fintan. A spot of reconnaissance. I see.

How long did you say you were in the game? asks the longhair.

Pastoral concerns? Oh, fifty years, give or take.

So, goes the hat. You'd know where all the bodies are buried out this way. Wouldn't be much got past an old hand like yourself.

Oh, says the old man, I don't take much of an interest anymore. Keep to myself, these days.

The billy rattles and steams. Fintan pushes his specs back up his nose. The afternoon sun hits the scaly top of his head and he's licking his lips like he's thinking hard and fast.

Nice and quiet out here, says the longhair.

It is indeed.

And just you out here these days is it? asks the hat.

Yes, yes, just me.

And then I catch them blokes looking at each other and it's like something's passed between them. And me heart fucking sinks like a brick. Because they're looking at me camo clobber and me shirt and socks all strung out on the wire. And I know sure as shit they've seen two pannikins on the sink inside and two greasy plates as well. Across the clearing, under the stubby gum, me swag's still unrolled and the sheets are all twisted up the way I climbed out of them this morning.

The driver in the hat walks over to the tree and checks out the dripping goat. At his feet a thousand greedy flies bubble and shine on the dirt. On the grey stump the knife and steel are layed down side by side. Fintan shuffles up near him with the longhair in behind and I can see his eyes like trapped fish in the bowls of his specs.

Well, says the hat. Gotta be a bit of a challenge living out here without a vehicle.

Fintan shrugs and opens his mouth.

Oh, says longhair, cutting him off. His mate's got that.

Whatsay?

I said your mate'll have the car, won't he?

No, no, says Fintan. There's no vehicle.

No kidding, says the hat.

I'm not even legal to drive, now, says the old man.

Not even a trail bike? says the longhair.

No, not even that. Strange as it may seem.

Well, you're a puzzle then, aren't you? says the hat.

A fountain of bullshit is what he is, says the longhair.

Ah, lads, I mystify myself, ye know. Now, how about that brew?

The poor old bugger never even saw the kick coming. And I only copped it at the last moment when longhair leant back and chopped him one in the kidney with his gay Adidas trainer. Like a karate thing it was, just a white flash you only saw after the old fella was already down on his hands and knees huffing and moaning. And then come another kick and the old man cried out, and the turd in the hat talked on, reasonable as anything.

I didn't make a sound. I don't think I was even breathing. I'm seeing all this close up, so tight in I can't get things focused in the scope anymore. And I'm doing exactly fuck all about it. I've still got the frigging safety on.

Righto, said the hat. Let's rewind. I'm in a hurry here. I don't have time for your piss-weak act. What's the deal here, Gramps?

How many of youse are there? said the longhair. What the fuck're youse up to?

Fintan felt about on the mucky dirt for his specs. I dunno if he had the wind to say anything but the longhair booted him again before he could.

Where's your phone?

No phone, said Fintan real quiet. No phone and no radio.

Go and look, said the hat to the hair.

Why don't you go and fuckin look?

Don't be a dick. Just check it out.

Jesus, said the hair, pulling away.

And I figured this was me best chance, now I had one of them cunts away from the other. I waited till the longhair was gone then I tried to wind the scope back for range but me hand was staked and me fingers were like they belonged on a stranger's hand and I could see the shadow of Fintan getting to his knees and the bloke with the hat lending an arm like he was some kind of civilized individual, one of nature's fucking gentlemen, and now I've gone and dialled the scope so far everything's a murky blur, so I'm futzing it back again when that longhaired bastard comes out and yells there's no bloody power, how can they run a phone out here with no fucking electricity?

Christ, said the hat. Haven't you boys heard of solar energy?

Oh, said Fintan, upright now, with his specs on again. Sure I have, now. And what a marvel it must be.

You should look into it, mate.

Well, said Fintan, a bit shaky. Note to self. Note to self, indeed.

Nah, said the hair. Him and his mates're too smart for that.

No batteries, said the hat. Not even a genny?

Ah, noisy divils, those generators. Never did like them.

He's old-school, this fella, said the hat. He's a hard case.

You lads seem to be several drinks ahead of me, said Fintan. I think I've lost the thread of the conversation somewhat.

Well, said the hat, it's probably best we clear this up quickly then.

He took up the knife and cut the goat off the gambrel. And that's when the old fella's face changed.

Get something to tie him with, said the hat.

My boy, said Fintan while the hair scrubbed round. You've come to the wrong place and the wrong man.

Is that a threat, Grandpa?

No, son, it's a simple statement of fact.

And I figured they were only bluffing him, that he'd see the guns and the gambrel and start telling them whatever it was they wanted to know, but when the longhair come out with a hank of barbwire I knew it wasn't gunna be like that.

They lashed him by the hands to the gambrel. He didn't struggle, he just nattered away like he thought they were ridiculous, like it was all a joke and a mistake. And all his chat must of got up them because the longhair hit him and his glasses bent and one side cracked. And he laughed, the mad game old bastard. His skin swam on him like it was too big for his carcase, like it was borrowed. With his hands up over his head like that he could of been a high diver getting ready to jump, or maybe a bloke stopping traffic. What he didn't look like was a man who was gunna surrender. Even if I wished to fuck he would.

They didn't hoist him off the ground these dumb cunts. I reckon they didn't know how. They just started poking at him with the blade, the knife I sharpened for him as a favour. Just a little at first, picking at him like it wasn't full serious. And they got into some song and dance about what we were up to, me and him, and got nowhere at all which is when they got real pissy and stepped it up.

And it was like all this was happening on telly. The shit they said and did. How weird and familiar it looked, horrible and not quite real. They're doing stuff to Fintan you wouldn't do to a mad dog. Like they're in some sicko vid even they can't believe is real. So you think in a sec it'll stop, this won't keep going, people don't really do this shit.

But there it is, they do it, keep at it, and you're stuck looking. Locked in watching. Because you can't truly believe in it. And you're filthy at yourself for letting it happen. With the blade you stoned up sharp as a motherfucker to show you're grateful without actually coming out and blabbing it.

It isn't like these shitheads are enjoying it, I'll give them that. Dude with the hat's jabbing his phone, stressing about no signal. And you can see pretty clear that now they got this circus going they don't know what to do about it, because the old boy's giving them jackshit and that's not what they were expecting. So they're scared now, frightened of themselves and feral with it. Digging Fintan with the knife tip, lifting his baggy grey skin, going on and on about his mate, about me, like where is he, because we got something to give him, something he left behind.

Over and over they went, on and on. Where was I? Who was I? What fucking was I?

And I don't know how to explain this, I'm not proud to be saying it, but I got caught up in it. Not the vicious shit, the cruel part or the streams of blood running off Fintan like he was some kid's painting. It was like I started wanting him to speak as much as those arseholes did. Maybe more. To make it stop. But also so I could know what Fintan really thought. About who I was. Maybe even what I was. All of a sudden this was deadly important. My heart was busting to know. And I wouldn't care if he did give me up. Christ, I wished he would. If only he'd say something true about me. It would be worth it just to hear. And that's the only excuse I can give for letting it go on so long. No one on this earth will ever understand this, I know, not even Lee, who knows me better than anyone alive or dead. But it's the truth, I got snagged up in the questions. And I was hanging on for his answers.

And the old man wouldn't say diddly squat. Half the time he looked happy, the cunning bugger. He was sly. And tougher than I could of imagined. I don't know if he knew I was there or not. If he couldn't see me or feel me then he musta believed he was on his own in the empty world and was just gunna die. But if he thought that, he never give a single sign of it. Not once. Not even when that longhaired fucker lost his shit and started cutting him for real. Fintan was high. Like he was tipsy with the fear and glad of the pain. Honest to God, he got bigger in the gambrel, straighter and stronger the longer it went on, and the way his skin got tight you'd swear he was filling up on something. The more they went at him, panicky and savage, the fuller and firmer and prouder he got. Fuck me dead, it was like he was grateful.

And then he caught me eye. Or maybe it was just a flash of sun off his busted up specs. He turned his head all round. Like a creature feeling the dark. And till that moment he was giving them nothing at all. But then he began to sing. Though it wasn't quite a song because he could only get it out in bits, in sucks of breath and groans. It come out in grunts like he was throwing it at them. But then I heard the words and I seen it was me he was throwing it at. In gobs and gargles he got a whole verse out. And that was plenty.

Oh, he fired. A shot at. Kelly. And laid him to the ground. And turning. Round to Da-aa-vis. He received . . . a fatal wound. A bullet pierced his brave young heart. From the pis-tol of Fitzroy. And that is how they cap-tured him. The Wild. Colonial. Boy?

Maybe he wanted me to kill him then. I've thought of that. A lot. Or it could be the song was just somewhere for him to go, like what I done a thousand times meself copping a flogging. It was always hard to tell with Fintan. The first time I heard him sing that song I wondered if he was singing it at me then too, taking the piss and geeing himself up all at once. Maybe it was just that again. But his eyes got so wide. Like he was running out of fun.

And they kept at him. Like they was out of ideas themselves. But they kept asking the three same questions.

Where was I?

Who was I?

What was I?

And for a long time Fintan took it just like that. Giving them nothing. And it was horrible and incredible and it all piled up on me, squashing me in, forcing me down, until something cracked and all in one moment it was like everything landed. All the birds landed. The sunlight landed. The song landed. All the decent things in him landed. On me. On my head. And I knew where I was, and who I was, and what I was. Yes, what I am. And it was just like he said. What I laughed at him for. It was like the sun and moon going through me. I was charged.

Then it all come out of me like a cough. I couldn't make it into words. But everything stopped. The whole fucking rigmarole. Even Fintan stopped. They all looked my way. There was piss running down the old man's legs. And then he wasn't looking at me anymore, his chin was on his chest and he give out a little coo. The world was silent, a quiet so deep that when the safety catch come off, the gritty sound the steel made was a shaming disgrace.

Fintan give a grunt then and sunk on the gambrel and the shithead with the hat reached behind for his automatic but I had the crosshair on his Adam's apple so when I fired I expected him to snap back like a roo. But the shot went wide and I thought I'd missed completely. Sounded like a misfire to me and I thought of all the dirt still in the barrel. The bloke stepped sideways a bit with his teeny little straw hat still on his head and that's when I saw the spout come out the side of him. Off the side of his neck. He sat down. Hawking and grabbing at himself. And when I turned the gun longhair's way that dumb evil cunt was just standing there with the knife. Looking down. At his mate. Like the dude didn't need any help at all. The fuckwit didn't even pull out his pistol.

The spent shell come out the .243 shining like a bright idea. And the second one went in sounding like bones grinding. The hair just couldn't credit what was happening. He didn't believe in me, that was it. But there I was.

I didn't say nothing. Though I could of. I had plenty to say but not to him. I saved it for Fintan. For now it was enough to know what I was. An instrument of God. And right at the last second the hair he knew it too. He turned to run and the back of his shirt ruffled where the first round struck him and he was halfway to the hut before he went down on his face. The second shot missed him totally and he crawled along a little way until I let another one loose and after a chunk come off the back of his head he give it up.

Fintan was breathing when I got to the gambrel. And he was still alive when I let him down on the sticky earth. I don't know if he heard anything I told him. There was spit running off his chin and his eyes looked half burst but I think he knew I was there. He felt me. He always knew what I was. He saw me coming before I knew I was even there. And now I saw him too.

I buried him on the lake, in the salt. It seemed right.

The others, they went in the mining business.

I never touched the weed. It wasn't worth the grief. But I did borrow the Jeep. And because of all the jerries in that horse float I've got enough petrol to get to Magnet and Broome and Darwin without having to stop. I've got almost everything I need. Food. Cash. A few books to remind me of Fintan. The rifle's gone of course. But there's a shotgun on the back seat. And a box of shells on the floor right here next to me.

Me phone's charged up now. No signal yet but I got to see her face at last. I'll be in Magnet by noon but I won't call till I'm just outside town. I'll take it slow with Lee. It'll all come pretty sudden, me showing up out of the blue, so I'll have to be patient. But I can afford to be. Because I know what I am now. And peace is on its way. It fucking better be.